Christmas in Whitcomb Springs

A WHITCOMB SPRINGS NOVELLA

MK MCCLINTOCK

About *Christmas in Whitcomb Springs*

"Hope is love's compass, reminding us that tomorrow's dawn can cradle the promise of a brighter beginning."

As snow blankets the mountain town of Whitcomb Springs, Montana, in 1867, a heartwarming story of love, hope, and second chances unfolds when Savannah and Hayes' paths intertwine with unexpected results. Perhaps this Christmas will bring more than just snow to Whitcomb Springs.

Christmas in Whitcomb Springs is a tale of resilience, second chances, and the transformative power of love that will warm your heart on even the coldest winter nights. This historical romantic Western will remind you of the miracles that can happen when love is rekindled amidst the snowy splendor of Christmas.

Copyright © 2024 by MK McClintock

Text by MK McClintock
Edited by Lorraine Fico-White

All rights reserved. Thank you for complying with copyright laws by not reproducing, scanning, or distributing any part of this work in any form without permission. If this book was purchased on an unauthorized platform, then it is a pirated and/or unauthorized copy and violators will be prosecuted to the full extent of the law. The publisher and author do not control and do not assume any responsibility for third-party websites or their content. For permission requests, write to the author via the contact page on the website below.

NO AI TRAINING: Without in any way limiting the author's exclusive rights under copyright, the author expressly prohibits any entity from using this publication to train AI technologies to generate text, including, without limitation, technologies capable of generating works in the same style or genre as this publication. The author reserves all rights to license uses of this work for generative AI training and development of machine learning language models.

Published by Trappers Peak Publishing in the United States of America

www.mkmcclintock.com

Publisher's Note: This is a work of fiction. Names, characters, places, and incidents are fictitious. Locales and public names are sometimes used for atmospheric purposes. Any resemblance to actual people, living or dead, or to businesses, companies, events, institutions, or locales is completely coincidental.

Christmas in Whitcomb Springs; novella/MK McClintock
Paperback ISBN: 979-8989985579

CHAPTER ONE

Frosty air nipped at Savannah Quinn's nose as puffs of breath swirled before her. She relished the brisk, chilly breeze that blew against her back and teased wisps of hair from the tightly knit wool cap she wore low enough to cover her ears. Once upon a time, six years and five months ago to be precise, she never would have worn a wool cap, let alone a thick scarf and woolen gloves, or had occasion to walk in snow that sometimes reached her knees.

Thanks to the industriousness of several men in Whitcomb Springs, the roads and porches in their mountain town remained clear enough for people to reach their destinations or to go outdoors and explore more of the place they called home.

Which is what Savannah did now. Wandering with little purpose except to see how far she could stroll into the meadow before the snow forced her to turn around and enjoy the frozen landscape from the comfort of her cozy cottage behind the clinic. The crunch of fresh snow beneath her boots echoed through the morning stillness, giving her a sense of peace and solitude in the wintry wonderland.

The morning sun, a pale orb visible through the gray winter clouds, cast a soft glow over the meadow, turning the snow into a blanket of diamonds. Savannah found her eyes drawn to the horizon, where the snowy peaks met the sky. There was a beauty here that she hadn't fully embraced during the early days after she left behind the bustling streets of Charleston seven months ago for the quiet, stark simplicity of Whitcomb Springs, Montana Territory.

It was, she had decided, the best decision she could have made for herself.

As she ventured farther, her thoughts drifted to Dr. Trevor Walker, whose steadfast presence had become a cornerstone in her new life. It was he who had offered her the position as a nurse in his clinic when she was at her lowest, believing that the healing powers of nature and the community would rejuvenate her weary spirit.

And indeed, they had.

"Savannah!"

She turned, smiled, and waved to Evelyn Whitcomb, a woman whose strength, kindness, and steadfastness had helped Savannah transition into her new life. She circled back and met Evelyn a dozen yards from her friend's front porch. "It is a glorious morning, and you look positively chilled."

"And you are out walking early. I thought we were to meet in an hour."

"Oh, we still are. It is only when I peered out the window and saw a glimpse of sun that I thought to enjoy an early walk." Savannah almost regretted losing the quiet time when she asked, "Would you like to join me now?"

In answer, Evelyn slipped her arm through Savannah's.

"I would. Daniel Jr. is still asleep, and his father is close should he awaken."

"How is his cold? Several of the children have suffered from it these past weeks."

"Much better, thank you. The tincture you gave us has worked." Evelyn stepped around a mess a horse left in the snow. "You haven't been this way in the snow yet, have you?"

"Not yet, though it is not knowing how deep the snow is in the meadow that has kept me away."

Evelyn gently led her farther left of where Savannah had walked. "If you keep in that direction, you will end up stepping in a smaller stream beneath the snow."

"Next you will tell me I should not be walking alone because I have done so many times as have you and many others."

"Not in winter."

Approaching a small copse of pines on the edge of town, between the Whitcomb's sprawling house and the open land beyond it, Savannah noticed tracks leading through the snow—a delicate pattern of tiny footprints weaving through the white. Curiosity piqued, they followed them, Savannah's heart lightening with each step, even as snow seeped over the top of her boots and her skirts dragged from the growing dampness. The trail led to a clearing where they spotted a trio of deer, their coats thick and brown against the snow. They lifted their heads to watch the two women approach but did not flee, as if they sensed their curiosity, rather than any danger.

"How charming! Oh, and look at these winter berries." Evelyn stepped away from Savannah, preoccupied now and not paying attention to her companion.

"Good morning," she whispered to the deer with a

gentle smile, feeling an inexplicable bond with the woodland creatures. Savannah stood still, observing them as they cautiously returned to rooting through the snow to reach the grass beneath, their breaths creating small puffs of steam in the cold air.

The scene's serenity stirred a deep contentment within her chest, a stark contrast to the turmoil she had felt upon her arrival in a place as far away from her previous home as she could find. Her reverie ended when she heard a sound similar to those she had spent far too many years listening for in the sick-infested wards of army hospitals.

She almost willed the sound away, telling herself it was merely a remnant of her former life sneaking upon her.

"Evelyn."

Evelyn turned, her smile faltering. "What is wrong?"

"Do you hear that noise?"

The low moan, this time accompanied by a series of deep-chested coughs, spurred Savannah forward, off the trail.

"Savannah, wait!"

More snow seeped into her boots, wetting her stockings, and her breathing became labored as she trudged through the snow, holding her skirt and petticoat above her knees so they wouldn't pull her down.

The noises stopped, and so did she. Savannah held her breath to hear something else besides it in the silence. When she felt her lungs near to bursting, another cough broke the quiet, and she released her breath before inhaling deeply. Savannah pivoted toward a small shelter of pines and dormant berry bushes, her legs growing weak.

"Savannah!"

Birds feasting on another shrub of winter berries scattered at her approach, fluttering into the sky before swooshing together once more in a taller pine tree. They would wait, she knew, until she'd left, before returning to their feast.

"Wait!" Evelyn caught up with her and pulled on her arm. "You do not know what is behind there."

"It is human, of that I am certain, and a sick or injured human."

"And your instinct, as would be mine, is to ensure their well-being." Evelyn exhaled and wiped her brow. "We go together."

Behind the bushes, and beneath a low-hanging bough of the closest tree, a man lay supine, his coughs producing intermittent streams of fog above his face. His legs and arms jerked a little with each cough, so at first glance did not appear broken. Savannah and Evelyn struggled through the snow until they reached the area closer to the trees, where the branches protected some of the ground from the taller drifts.

Savannah stumbled to the ground next to the man, the snow and fallen pine needles creating a soft enough blanket for her knees. She barely kept her upper body from landing on him and braced herself with her arms until her torso was hovering over his. "All right. We are good. All you need, sir, is my clumsiness, causing further injury." Releasing a quick breath, she pushed herself back to sit on her heels. "Can you hear me?"

Evelyn kneeled on the man's other side. "We need help."

Savannah gave him a cursory study from head to boots, and roving back up his body, her eyes fixated on a darker section of his black shirt—too dark to be wet only from the snow. She recognized the spread pattern and how it had stopped spreading thanks to the cold, which likely meant the wound had stopped bleeding. Worse, though, that the shirt was probably stiff and stuck to the wound.

"Savannah, we are not strong enough to lift him or carry him ourselves. He may as well be dead before we can bring help."

Savannah cupped the man's strong jaw, her palm brushing against at least two days' worth of whiskers. "Can you please open your eyes so I know you will not die on me?"

"I can hear you."

Savannah barely heard his whisper, and thankfully he did not sound as though his lungs held fluid. "That is good. Great." She looked up at Evelyn. "Can you go for help?"

Evelyn shook her head. "I am not leaving you alone."

"He is hardly in any condition to be of any danger to me." Savannah's hands moved into his hair, checking all over his scalp for wounds. Her heartbeats slowed enough for her to think clearer once she found no head wounds. "If talking hurts, sir, can you blink in response to my questions?"

In answer, the man's eyelids fluttered open. Savannah noted the long, dark lashes, which she really shouldn't have. His wound and figuring out how to get him back to town were all that mattered. Truly, though, they were beautiful lashes for a man and the soft green eyes they slowly unveiled even more so.

"Do you have only the wound in your side?"

He blinked once. Since she had forgotten to indicate blink once or twice for yes or no, she asked, "Does that mean yes? One blink, that is?"

He blinked once again. Savannah took that as confirmation.

"It doesn't hurt to talk." He coughed again. "Much."

"Laying down is going to make the cough worse." Though she had nothing to remedy the situation. She surveyed their surroundings and saw no horse or other mode of transportation. Savannah knew that the nearby trails would all be covered in snow, and she knew that there were more trails, water, and mountains beyond the meadow.

"Savannah, look."

Her gaze followed where Evelyn pointed and stopped on tracks four or maybe five feet away on the other side of the tree's base. Blood spots stained the surrounding snow. She exchanged a fleeting and worried glance with her friend before returning her attention back to the man.

"You made it this far. If I wrap the wound, do you think you can walk with us back to town?"

Those wonderful moss-green eyes—somehow familiar—met her gaze. His eyes shifted, moving up and down, giving her a longer study than she had him. "I have no idea."

"I am stronger than I look." She'd learned to be—had to be. Savannah had lifted wounded men when they'd fallen over, turned their bodies to change bandages, and raised them up from their cots to help them eat or use the necessary. Yes, she'd learned to be strong. "If you can find it in yourself to go a little farther, there is a doctor in town who can help you. A wonderful doctor."

"If you will allow me." Savannah pointed to his shirt to indicate what she meant to do. The man nodded. "What is your name?" she asked as she untucked the hem of his shirt and raised it enough to reach the union suit beneath.

"Munro."

"A good, stalwart name, and imagine you can lay claim fierce warriors as ancestors." Savannah kept up the conversation as she removed her gloves and warmed her hands by rubbing them together, the skin tingling as blood rushed to the tips. "I knew a family of Munros, a long time ago. Wonderful people." She prodded the area around the wound. Surprised when the fabric pulled up with less resistance than she had expected, Savannah inspected the injury.

"This is from a bullet, Mr. Munro." Her fingers probed underneath his coat and found an exit wound where the fabric was sticking to the skin. "I am going to wrap this the best I can. It might bleed again, but there is no help for it. By the time we get back to town on our own and return with help, the animals will have found you, or you'll have frozen near to death. You are cold, but not so cold that you have been out here too long yet." Savannah almost forgot about Evelyn as she tried to tear a strip from her sturdy petticoat, but the fabric wouldn't give under her stiff fingers.

"In my boot."

Savannah stared at his face, then dragged her gaze to his boot. Raising the pant leg above the boot, she found a blade handle protruding. "That always seemed rather a dangerous practice. I should think it an easy way to lose a foot." Not expecting a response, she withdrew the knife, somewhat taken aback by its six well-sharpened inches. The tip sliced easily through the petticoat, and in no time, she had cut two strips. One she folded over and pressed against the front wound. Evelyn took the knife and cut a portion of her petticoat as well, handing the fabric back to Savannah and slipping the knife back into the man's boot.

"I need to lift you enough to tie this around your torso, beneath your coat. Can you manage, Mr. Munro?"

Savannah asked, even as she moved her arm beneath his shoulder.

He surprised her by lifting his upper body easily with Evelyn's help, though his right hand quickly went to the wound, and Savannah caught the quick wince of pain on his face. "I'll stay up."

Believing him, Savannah wrapped the longer strip of fabric around his waist, grateful she had enough. Had the wound been higher, nearer the upper chest, she wouldn't have had enough petticoat without tying pieces together. "It should hold, I hope, for a short while." She looked up at the sky. "By now, there will be others about, and with luck, they will see us before we reach the edge of town."

She lowered his shirt, leaving the ends untucked. "Do you think you can stand if we each give you a shoulder?"

He nodded. Savannah first helped him to his knees, telling him to use her shoulder as leverage. Then he got to his feet. Savannah struggled to hers, shocked when he took some of her weight until she stood. Evelyn slipped beneath his other shoulder.

"Nothing's wrong with my legs, but I can't say how much blood I lost getting this far. It will be safer for you if . . ." He stopped, his body wracked with coughs.

"My name is Savannah Quinn, Mr. Munro." She swore a twinkle flashed in his eyes. There was no mistaking the pained smile he gave her. "And this is Evelyn Whitcomb."

"Not safe out here for ladies. I can rest upright against the tree while you two go on back without me."

Even before he finished speaking, Savannah was shaking her head and wrapping her arm around his waist. "I do not recall suggesting such an option. A few stout men might assist you better, but certainly not carry you. They could bring a sleigh, though, as I said—"

"I'll be dead before they get here."

She peered at his face and noted the firm lines and the tightened jaw. "Your cough seems to have eased, though I suspect that was because of your fall and the way you were lying."

"I am not at risk of a lung ailment, if that concerns you, Miss Quinn."

"No, though I daresay wolves will find you a tempting meal, which concerns me a good deal, Mr. Munro."

As though on cue, and to prove her point, a distant howl, followed by another, drifted through the air.

"For you, Miss Quinn, I can make it."

They stopped to rest after what Savannah estimated to be about twenty minutes. She had not realized how far into the meadow she and Evelyn had ventured, and seeing their original tracks in the snow now, she did not know how she'd ever heard him. Sunrise came late in winter, and based on the sun and when she left her cabin, she guessed an hour or more had passed since she ventured outdoors.

"Evelyn, you should go ahead without us and bring help." Before Evelyn could shake her head, Savannah added, "Please. You can move faster on your own, and truly, I will be safe."

Mr. Munro nodded. "She'll be safe, though I understand your reluctance."

Evelyn removed his arm from around her shoulder. "I do not know why we should trust you, Mr. Munro, and understand I am doing this for her, not you."

"Understood." Hayes leaned a little heavier on Savannah before righting himself.

To Savannah, Evelyn said, "I will hurry," before rushing toward town, her skirts dragging over the snow's surface.

"What were you doing out here?"

"Walking. Though I stay closer to town when on my own." Savannah brushed the dark strands of hair that had fallen out from under her wool hat from the exertions. "And yourself, Mr. Munro? How did you end up with a bullet passing through you and no horse?"

He grasped his middle and raised his face to the sky, breathed deeply, and looked at her. "I fell off my horse when the bullet hit me. As to why it happened, I'd also like to know, Miss Quinn."

"Well, there will be time enough for more questions later." She wrapped her arm once more around his waist, grateful for his height. Savannah had always been tall for a female at five feet, eight inches, but her shoulder fit neatly beneath his arm, allowing her to walk without hunching. "I am certain we are close."

"We are."

"Oh?" She stopped again and stared at him. "Have you been to Whitcomb Springs before?"

He shook his head and jutted his chin a little forward and upward. "Smoke's rising from chimneys."

Savannah followed his gaze and indeed saw smoke swirling into the air—several streams of them. "I will admit to some relief. It was not so cold when I left the cabin this morning." Neither of them mentioned she was now missing part of her petticoat and, with it gone, an extra layer of warmth. "Not too far to the Whitcomb's house. Daniel—he is Evelyn's husband—has a sleigh that will take you the rest of the way to the clinic."

"Whitcomb, as in the town?"

Savannah nodded. Talking took her mind off the

struggle to walk, though she noticed less weight on her shoulder than when they first started. "Daniel and Evelyn Whitcomb founded the town. They came out here before the war, and then Daniel enlisted. Evelyn stuck it out here on her own; well, not alone because others remained, and more have arrived since the war ended. There's mining and timber." She halted unexpectedly. "I just need to catch my breath." She used the rest as an excuse to check his wound. Her once-white petticoat was now stained with fresh blood. "We are close enough now for you to wait while I get help, and I haven't heard the wolves for at least ten minutes."

In response to her idea, he crumbled to the earth and sank into the snow.

CHAPTER TWO

Hayes Munro had always believed in a life beyond the one on Earth. He imagined a peaceful place where people lived without pain, wars ceased to plague humanity, and the woman he bound himself to on Earth would be bound to him in Heaven.

He recalled, recently, an excruciating pain in his side where the bullet had pierced his skin and thankfully escaped through his back. Hayes remembered the cold, the cough, and the howl of wolves somewhere in the great, beautiful expanse of a snow-covered landscape he'd been admiring before someone shot him off his horse.

Now, with the pain gone, warm air all around, and the sweet scent of flowers, he guessed the bullet had done more harm than he first thought. He only wished he'd had more time with Miss Savannah Quinn before the good lord saw fit to take him away.

"Mr. Munro?"

Hayes smiled at the sweetest sound his ears had ever

heard. "I'm not dead." He frowned a little at the weakness in his voice.

"No, you're not dead. Better than that, the doctor expects you to fully recover."

His eyes opened and slowly focused on the angelic face above him. Hayes expected he owed someone a great deal for the second chance, and he always repaid his debts. "How long have I been out?"

"Four hours and twelve minutes." He felt her gentle fingers on his shoulder as she glanced at something across the room. "Make that thirteen minutes."

His brow raised. "Accurate."

She did not respond to what was obviously not a question. "Dr. Walker stitched you up nicely. He also said you lost a lot of blood and must rest for a few days before exerting yourself. There's a room with a comfortable bed here in the clinic where we can look after you while your wound heals. You need to focus on regaining your strength."

Hayes watched her inspect his wound and then move around the clinic like she knew what she was doing. "How long have you been a nurse?"

Her hands stilled. One held a fresh cloth, the other a pair of scissors. "Since Vicksburg." Her tone did not invite further inquiry as she deftly changed his bandage and tossed the soiled one into a bowl. "What brings you to Whitcomb Springs, Mr. Munro?"

When she finished covering him again with a blanket, he clasped her hand. "It's Hayes. Hayes Munro."

Savannah's gaze shifted quickly to his face. He gave her time to study him, knowing he'd changed a good deal from the fifteen-year-old she'd once known. Twelve years of living, a foot in height, a lot of muscle, and four years of war had transformed the youth she once knew into the man who'd come looking for her.

"Hayes."

"It's been a long time, Savannah."

She kept her hands on his arm. "Your name appeared on the rolls of those captured at Vicksburg." Her fingers shook now even as she kept her voice clear and strong. "Were the reports wrong?"

Hayes pushed himself upward, and Savannah quickly tucked another pillow beneath his shoulders.

"You shouldn't be sitting up yet."

"I don't want to have this conversation with me flat on my back." His voice no longer carried a hint of the southern youth she once called a friend, before her father packed up their belongings and the family and relocated to Vermont. He remembered their goodbye, the sweet kiss placed at the corner of his mouth before she rushed away. He also recalled too well her father's determination to keep them apart.

For eight years, he had thought of little else except Savannah Quinn, for thoughts of her prevented him from considering marriage when he should have, and eventually the memory of his love for her carried him through the harshness of war.

Pain had kept him from studying her the way he wanted to out in the icy cold. Now, in the clinic's warmth, his gaze roamed freely. Hayes would have recognized her anywhere, for unlike him, she had changed little from the pretty young woman he'd once dreamed of marrying. Her warm, expressive eyes had always revealed every emotion, and her thick sable hair, which he remembered she used to wear loosely around her shoulders or in a single braid tied off with a ribbon. She wore her hair now bundled in a soft knot atop her head.

Still, he would have recognized her anywhere.

"The reports were not wrong," he finally said, each word measured like the drops of rain that sometimes preceded a storm on the horizon. "But fate, it seems, had a different plan for me."

She reluctantly released his arm and stood back, folding her hands to still their trembling. "A different plan," she repeated softly, more to herself than to him. Savannah looked away toward the frosty windows.

"Yes," Hayes continued, shifting slightly. "After Vicksburg, I was taken prisoner. The march to the camp . . . men died from exhaustion, hunger . . . despair." His gaze drifted past her, perhaps seeing again those dark days. "Thinking of you kept me sane and determined to survive. I lost track of you, Savannah, after your second year in Vermont. The letters I sent always came back."

Savannah caused a twinge in her neck with the sudden shift of her head to look at him again. "I received no letters—my father."

Hayes didn't voice his agreement.

She hesitated, her eyes scanning his face for signs of the man she remembered, the one who had left with promises wrapped in hope and sealed with youthful passion. No other had she kissed in her lifetime, so the memory of Hayes's kiss remained imprinted even after all these years.

"We returned to South Carolina in 1861, after my father died. My mother wanted to be closer to her family, and no one expected the war to become the four years of fire, fury, and death we all suffered through." Savannah rested her palm on his hand. "You had already enlisted to fight for the Union."

"You knew?"

Savannah nodded. "Your letters didn't reach me, but others in Charleston kept me informed. Our old pastor's wife wrote my mother monthly. I was proud of your decision, though I never could say such things in front of my mother. She hated the war years and wasn't fond of what she called 'Northern ways and thinking' by the time we left."

"Did you dislike living up north?"

"I missed the mountains and the crisp air of Vermont after we returned to the sweltering heat of South Carolina, so no, I did not hate it. Vermont, then my father's death, and then . . . well, the war only made living with my mother more difficult, like a wound that wouldn't heal. Leaving and coming here was a relief."

He observed her as she worked, the way her neck curved when she leaned forward and the brief, almost imperceptible glances she sent him before returning to her tasks. "I never imagined I'd find you here, tucked away from the world, in a town barely marked on any map."

Savannah turned back to him. "Nor did I think I'd ever see you again, not after hearing about the constant battles and losses." Her voice trembled slightly as she continued. "Sometimes I thought it was a mercy I didn't know whether you lived or died. The not knowing meant there was always hope." Her eyes met his. "We were so young when my family moved, and I never imagined you would remember me. Why are you here, Hayes Munro?"

Hayes raised his arm, the one not held against his body in a sling, and cupped her cheek against his palm. "First, to find you, Savannah Quinn."

The clinic's front door opened enough to allow entry to Dr. Walker. He brought with him a burst of cold, which he quickly stifled when he shut the door while balancing a rectangular wooden box Savannah knew held a tray with Hayes's meal.

Savannah left Hayes's side and hurried to help the doctor after he set the box down on a long table by the window.

"There are two meals in there, Miss Quinn. One for you. You haven't left our patient since the surgery." Dr. Walker stuffed his gloves into his coat pocket and removed it and a thick scarf, hanging them on hooks by the door before approaching Hayes. If he had witnessed anything between his patient and nurse, he politely kept it to himself.

"It's heartening to see you awake, Mr. Munro. However, I'd like it better if you were lying down. You'll ruin my stitches." Dr. Walker checked Hayes's vitals. "How long have you been awake?"

"Not long," Hayes answered before Savannah could. "And long enough."

Dr. Walker smiled and turned to Savannah. "Miss Quinn. Would you please place the supply order at the general store while I finish my examination of our patient? There's no wind right now, and I always recommend fresh air. I've added two items to your list. The food won't go cold."

Savannah eyed both men, then murmured, "Of course," before gathering her wool cloak, scarf, and hat. She was slipping her hands into gloves when she grabbed a sheet of paper off the desk and left the clinic.

Dr. Walker tapped his shoulder and stood next to Hayes's uninjured side. "Lean on me. There's a privy attached to the back of the clinic. I'll walk you as far as the door."

Once Hayes returned to the clinic's main room and used the water, soap, and clean cloths the doctor had set out, Dr. Walker helped him into a chair rather than back on the examination table. Hayes wished he could walk farther, out into the cold and back through the meadow to find his horse.

"It's been a while since we've had an injured stranger in Whitcomb Springs." Dr. Walker leaned against the examination table. Hayes had noticed the doctor was almost as tall as himself, with eyes nearly as dark as his hair. He kept his face clean-shaven, which reminded Hayes it had been too long since he'd shaved the whiskers from his face.

No wonder Savannah hadn't recognized him. Hayes studied the doctor and wondered if the man had ever attempted to court Savannah. "Not a stranger, exactly."

"Yes, I saw you and Miss Quinn through the window before I came in. She cares about her patients, though not so much care as she has shown you." Dr. Walker crossed his arms and looked at Hayes, much like he imagined a brother would have—if Savannah had a brother. "How do you know her?"

"You should ask her if she wants to tell anyone."

"I'm asking you, Mr. Munro."

"The name is Hayes, and Savannah and I—"

Dr. Walker held up a hand. "I have it now. Consider me like her older and very protective brother, Mr. Munro, and understand that I won't tolerate anyone—even you— hurting her."

"Since you seem to know who I am, you know I'd never cause her harm. She obviously spoke of me."

"Call me Taylor. Most folks around here do. And no, she didn't speak of you, at least not that she's aware."

Hayes eased his body forward, felt a tug on the stitches, and eased back. "What do you mean?"

Taylor shook his head. "She will tell you her story if she wants to. Suffice to say, if you came here to find her, I need to know how you ended up—"

"Hold on." Ignoring the tug this time, and Taylor's raised brow, Hayes sat forward. "I don't know who shot me. As soon as my wound heals enough, I intend to find out."

"Do you know then why someone shot you?" Taylor pressed.

"I followed smoke to a campfire on the other side of the ridge. Whoever had been there hadn't packed up the camp yet. I was still on my horse when the first shot went by, missed. The second shot hit me. I rode for a while and at some point, lost consciousness. You know the rest." Hayes met Taylor's stare, doing his best to keep his face from expressing the pain his wound was giving him.

Taylor broke the silence. "But you're here to find Miss Quinn?"

Hayes nodded. "She's why I came to Whitcomb Springs."

Taylor studied him again. "That's not exactly an answer."

"I'm grateful to you for saving my life, Dr. Walker—"

"Taylor."

"I'm grateful," Hayes repeated. "And I expect we could even be friends so long as you're not as nosy as you've been in the last five minutes. I came to the territory to find

Savannah. Upon arriving, I learned someone else I know is living here. Obligations mean finding him as well."

"Why would someone want to shoot you?"

"Since no one save one person in South Carolina knows I'm here, it does me no good to speculate except to say someone clearly did not want me at their camp." Hayes adjusted his frame in the chair and gritted his teeth against the pain in his side. "I expected to meet your sheriff by now."

"You could if he was here." Taylor walked to a tall cabinet with lead-plated glass panes closed over half a dozen shelves above a long workbench. He took out a bottle of white powder from off the far-left shelf, mixed some in a glass of water, and crossed the room again to give it to Hayes. "Drink this down. It will help with the pain."

Hayes eyed the opaque water with its unappetizing bits of power on the surface and deciding to trust the doctor, drank it in two swallows. "It goes down better than I expected."

"I'll give you another glass this evening. You'll be confined to the bed in the back room for a day, maybe two, and then you can go to the hotel. It's a small hotel, and a young family who lost their house last week is taking up two rooms, but I expect they have a room to spare. I've been told people rarely visit this time of year."

Hayes admired the doctor's not-so-subtle and roundabout way of asking a question. "I wouldn't expect so, with the pass barely passable and the road flattened enough only, it seems, for a sleigh." He rested his head against the chair's top rail. "I came up with the supply sleigh. We reached about three miles outside of town before the grizzled man I paid ten dollars to give me a spot on the sleigh's bench stopped at a way station or rather a farm. He planned on staying there until the cold front passed. I bought a horse from the farmer and took the deer trail through the woods. Hardly any snow."

Taylor studied him for a full minute before saying, "You and Miss Quinn must have quite a history."

The doctor cut off the conversation when the clinic door swung open and a chilly wind entered with Savannah. "The wind has picked back up. I've placed the order, and what they had on hand, one of the Stockman boys will deliver later today. It's Ben Stockman's turn this week at the store, and his brother is running messages to and from the mine." She brushed snow off her shoulders and removed her hat, though kept her cloak and gloves on while her gaze darted between the men. "Have I interrupted?"

Taylor shook his head, passed Savannah, and donned his outer clothing before reaching for a brown leather medical bag on a bench beside the door. "I promised Mrs. Pruitt I'd be by today to check on her son's cough. Be sure to eat, both of you."

Savannah removed her cloak and gloves and slipped the straps of a crisp white apron over her arms. She watched Hayes while she tied the fabric ends at the back of her waist. "What was that about?"

"That?"

Her mouth twisted a little. "You know well enough what I mean, Hayes Munro. You and Dr. Walker. When I entered, the air hummed with male tension, though I was too cold at first to notice. I spent enough time with soldiers to recognize the signs."

"Dr. Walker was a soldier?"

"Mm. He was a physician in the field hospitals."

Seeing no need not to tell her the truth, Hayes said,

"He wants to be sure my intentions are honorable where you're concerned."

Savannah dropped her arms to her side and stared at him. "Why would he think you have any intentions?"

Hayes's brow arched up.

"Yes, you said you came here to find me, and we'll get to that soon enough. What did you tell Dr. Walker?"

"Do you always call him Dr. Walker, or do you ever call him Taylor?" Hayes shrugged and regretted the slight pull on his stitches. "He told me to call him Taylor."

Savannah's eyes softened, a gentle hue enveloping them as she considered Hayes' question. "Taylor has always been Dr. Walker to me," she said slowly, as if realizing the distance the title created between them for the first time. "He's been like a brother since my arrival. He looks out for me more than I sometimes think necessary."

Hayes nodded, understanding the protective instincts, and absurdly grateful she had said "brother" in her description of him. The sun began descending behind the mountains, casting long shadows through the window. "He seemed to think I might threaten your well-being."

"That sounds like him." Savannah lit the wicks on two oil lamps. "It gets dark early here in the winter. Dr. Walker . . . Taylor tends to see danger in every shadow, especially when it comes to me."

"Perhaps because he knows what shadows can hide," Hayes suggested, his voice low. His own past was a vivid testament to that truth—hidden memories and unspoken fears that shaped his guarded nature.

Savannah looked at him then, really looked, as if trying to peer through the facade everyone wears and see the person beneath. "And what about you, Hayes Munro? The shadows you are hiding from must be ferocious to have sent you so far from home."

Hayes felt an unexpected surge of vulnerability under her scrutiny. When he didn't answer right away, she crossed her arms and matched his stare. "Did you know I was here when you set out for the territory?"

"You're too suspicious." He smiled. Childn't help it. "Yes, I knew." Hayes sobered and adjusted himself in the chair. Whatever Dr. Walker had given him had eased the pain some. Except, without the pain to keep him lucid, sleep fought to drag him back under. "Before you ask what I think might be your next question, no, you're not the only reason I'm here, at least not now."

Hayes reached for her hand, grasped it, ignoring the tug on his injury. "I would have come, no matter what, to find you first. I need you to know that."

Savannah stepped closer, allowing his arm to rest on his lap. She did not try to free her hand from his gentle grip. "What is the other reason you're here?"

"All right, we'll talk about that first." Hayes rubbed his thumb over the back of her hand before letting go, resting his head, and fighting back sleep. "My brother."

Her brow furrowed, and she shook her head. "I don't recall you having a brother."

"You never met him. Elijah's a year younger than me and spent six months of each year with our uncle—my mother's older brother—over several years. My mother hoped Elijah would become a doctor. Our uncle was a physician who later joined the Union Army and helped open the hospital in Hilton Head. Elijah cared little about doctoring and spent whatever time he could in the forests and by the sea, where he often disappeared for hours, dreaming of far-off places. He left South Carolina after the war ended and like many, wanted to find gold in Montana Territory. Elijah wrote to me before he left and every few months since. It's been five months since I last heard from him."

"Did he serve?"

Hayes nodded. "Two years in the Confederate Army as a clerk in Richmond and thankfully, never saw combat."

Savannah pulled another chair closer to Hayes and lowered herself into it. "How did you know he was here?"

Hayes's throat burned, and before he could ask for water, Savannah had risen, filled a glass from a stoneware pitcher, and held the glass in front of him. He thanked her, and after drinking half the water, he answered her question. "A man I served with came out here with Elijah. Last month, he sent word that my brother had fallen in with a group of men suspected of causing trouble between Butte and Cheyenne." Hayes finished the water and Savannah took the glass from him before he set it down. "I had already purchased my train ticket to St. Louis when I received the letter."

"You mean you were already coming here to find me?"

Hayes nodded. "I visited your mother's grave."

Savannah's expression softened. "She always liked you."

"She wanted better for you than me," Hayes corrected.

"My father did. Foremost, my mother wanted me to be happy."

"Were you happy?" Hayes didn't realize how important her answer was to him until that moment.

"Briefly. I tried to convince myself Charleston was home, only there was nothing left for me there."

"How did you choose this place?"

Savannah smiled. "Evelyn Whitcomb's sister, Abigail. Abigail McCord now. One of her society friends from up north lived in Charleston after the war with her husband. We both volunteered for a charity helping wounded soldiers. She shared stories from Abigail's letters. It took a little time to gather the courage to travel so far." She stood and crossed the room to the window, giving her back to Hayes. "And it took time to accept that you might not return from the war."

Cursing his injury and ignoring both exhaustion and twinges of pain, Hayes pushed himself up from the chair, steadied his legs, and joined her at the window.

"How did you know?"

Hayes didn't have to ask what she meant. "Mrs. Pennybaker."

A laugh escaped Savannah's lips and reached his ears. It was, to Hayes's thinking, the sweetest sound he'd ever heard.

"I am certain Mrs. Pennybaker would have adopted you if she and her husband hadn't already raised two sons. I remember she used to sneak you candy when her husband wasn't looking."

"She remembered, too." Hayes ached to reach out and glide his fingers through the silky softness of her hair. He checked himself. "The Pennybakers sold their general store but still live in the house next to it. She told me where you'd gone."

"I thought someone should know." Savannah shrugged and finally turned back to face him. "Leaving everything I knew behind wasn't as difficult as I imagined, and yet, after I purchased my ticket, I wanted to tell someone, just because."

"What did you do after St. Louis, Savannah? How did you get here?"

"The same way others have before me. Train, steamboat, stagecoach, then wagon."

"By yourself?"

She raised her brow again. He admired her ability to convey many words with one smooth arch.

"Yes, I also came here by myself, and before this becomes an argument on what women should and shouldn't do, or what men should and shouldn't tell women to do," he quickly added, "my question is still valid."

"Yes, by myself. As it happens, though, a group of missionaries were traveling here, three kindly couples, and after St. Louis, I journeyed with them as far as Bozeman, where I disembarked. After what I witnessed on the battlefields and in the hospitals, the journey to Whitcomb Springs was rather a holiday, and the scenery spectacular, the weather fair. I never imagined such places existed."

Hayes gave in to the urge and gently brushed his palm over her hair before cupping her cheek. "I'm sorry you endured any of the war."

"You endured worse." Her eyes shuttered momentarily, and she held her hand over his. "Hayes, I'm glad you are here."

Had he not been watching her face, the gentle parting of her lips as she exhaled soft breaths, he might have missed her barely whispered words. Hayes felt a stirring deep within him, a longing tempered by the fires of war, imprisonment, and the possibility that he'd lost Savannah Quinn forever. He no longer saw a reason to temper anything.

"It matters not what I've been through. I voluntarily enlisted and understood the risks." His voice barely rose above the whisper of the wind outside. "It's where I am and who I'm with now that matters." His thumb traced the line of her jaw tenderly, his touch tentative as if he feared they might both awaken to find it all a dream.

A small smile tugged at the corners of her mouth, lighting up her features with a warmth that reached her eyes. "And where is that?" she asked, her tone teasing yet laden with an emotion he couldn't quite discern.

"Here, with you," Hayes replied, his words simple but charged with an earnestness that tightened his chest.

She leaned into his touch, closing the distance between them until their foreheads touched. "What of your brother?"

Hayes eased back and studied her, wondering at the shift in her mood, and then understanding. "The only way I'm leaving you is if you push me out the door and out of your life." He gave his words a moment to register before he answered her question. "I don't know where Elijah is. The letter I received said he was last in Butte."

"How can I help?"

Now it was Hayes's turn to raise a brow. "I hope you mean help as in moral support because any other help is not an option. There's no telling what trouble Elijah has found himself in, and I won't risk your safety, not even to rescue him."

"I did not intend to brandish a weapon and ride, as you did, through heavy snow to risk my life. Come." She ushered him back to the chair where she not quite, but close, forced him down. "Dr. Walker will be displeased with your exertions."

"I'm surprised he's left us alone this long."

"You are a patient and I am a nurse, nor are you in any condition to cause me too many problems." She smirked at him. "He also lives upstairs, though a house call or dinner invitation often waylays him. There are still several single women in town, and a few have their sights set on our doctor."

Hayes had to ask. "Not you, though."

"No, not me." Savannah smiled as she removed the tray with two meals from the protective box and unwrapped the white cloth covering each plate. "Still warm, barely." She scooted a small table in front of Hayes and set the plates on the polished surface. "Meatloaf sandwiches and applesauce. Lucky for us, the café's meatloaf sandwiches are delicious, even when cool."

She refilled his water glass and filled one for herself. "Now, let's discuss how I can assist you in your quest. Some of the townsfolk keep up with rumblings in areas farther away. Trouble has a way of echoing through these parts. Cooper McCord is where we'll start."

"Evelyn Whitcomb's brother-in-law?"

Savannah nodded. "Cooper and Abigail returned from a visit to Boston right before the first snowfall to ensure they'd be here for Christmas. He was the guide who first brought Daniel and Evelyn Whitcomb to this valley. If there is trouble brewing, he'll have heard about it."

Hayes watched her closely, studying the sincerity etched across her features. The warm glow from the oil lamp painted shadows on her face, accentuating her resolve. "I won't put you in any danger."

"As I have already pointed out, Hayes, I've been in far worse danger." Savannah's voice held a note of quiet strength that kept Hayes's gaze on her a moment longer. "And besides, helping people is what I do. Whether it's mending broken bodies, spirits, or in your case, helping you find your brother."

Hayes's gaze followed her as she walked to the cast-iron stove, fed the fire, and set a kettle on a burner. "All right," he conceded, his voice barely above a whisper. "We'll go see Cooper tomorrow. But promise me, Savannah, if—"

"Introducing you to Cooper and a few others and helping glean information will not endanger me." Her chin lifted slightly when she returned to the table and picked up half her sandwich. "Now, eat. Dr. Walker will expect clean plates when he returns."

CHAPTER THREE

Savannah stared out her cabin window and unwound her braid. The clouds had cleared away, leaving a cascade of stars splashed against an inky sky. She peered upward through the window, between the cabin and a stand of stalwart aspens bereft of leaves, and thought of Hayes.

The hours devoted to thinking of Hayes Munro had multiplied exponentially since she said farewell to him all those years ago. Still young and optimistic, before war and death had changed how she viewed life, she had longed for no one more than Hayes.

The fire crackled behind her, sending a shower of sparks up the chimney. Outside, the wind howled, a mournful sound that seemed to echo the tumult of emotions swirling within her. Snow was falling heavily now, blanketing the world in white. Savannah sighed, her breath fogging the glass. She traced a delicate pattern on the windowpane, her fingers leaving ghostly trails in the condensation.

"Hayes Munro," she whispered, tasting the longing of his name on her lips.

A gust of wind rattled the cabin, causing Savannah to start. She turned from the window, closed the curtains, and wrapped her shawl tighter around her shoulders. The fire's warmth beckoned, and she moved closer, seeking comfort in its amber glow.

The logs shifted in the hearth, sending up another spray of sparks. Savannah watched them dance, her mind drifting to the day she'd last seen Hayes in South Carolina.

"We'll find each other again one day," he had promised, his voice full of youthful conviction. "We'll build a life together, Savannah. You'll see."

But the years had stretched, and they had not found each other. The war came and went, leaving scars on the land and in people's hearts. Savannah had thrown herself into her work as a nurse, finding solace in healing. Yet even as she tended to the wounds of others, her own heart remained raw and aching.

Her eyes scanned the cabin interior, devoid of the usual trimmings she would normally have hung around her house the first week of December. Tomorrow, she planned to gather greens for garland and wreaths, search for the winterberry bushes Evelyn Whitcomb said grew in abundance behind their house, and perhaps buy a few new beeswax candles from the general store for the mantel.

Christmas had been her favorite time of year before the war. In the years during the war, she joined other nurses to make the holiday special for soldiers, but without home and family, uplifting spirits became exhausting.

Savannah settled into the rocking chair by the hearth, allowing her mind to wander back to a time she wished she could forget.

After the war, she had tried and failed to bring to life Christmases like before the war years. And now, here she was, allowing another December to pass without the nostalgic sights of holiday decorations or the cozy feel of a soft wool between her fingers for the knitted scarves she always made for her mother and father. She was now determined to prevent the past from dampening the Christmas season.

Perhaps Hayes would like a scarf.

A sudden knock at the door startled her from her reverie. Savannah hesitated, her brow furrowing. She stared at the bar across the door as it rattled a little against its iron braces. Savannah walked toward the door, stopping four feet short of it. "Who is it?"

Silence met her question.

Unless someone approached Whitcomb Springs from the small woods behind her cabin, hers was not the first house from any direction. Savannah's heart quickened, a chill creeping up her spine despite the warmth of the hearth fire. Her fingers curled around the rough-hewn wood of a nearby chair for support. "Is anyone there?"

Again, silence. Savannah thought of the side door, also barred from the inside. A few steps out her door and she could be at the clinic.

The knocking sounded again, this time from her side door. Savannah did what she hadn't since her arrival, since Daniel and Evelyn Whitcomb presented her with a pistol she kept in a box on a shelf in her small living room. She took down the box, opened the lid, and lifted the pistol into her hand. Daniel had told her the model and caliber and showed her how to load it. She kept it loaded and unused since she first put it away.

Savannah had never wanted to learn how to use a gun,

having seen enough of their damage during the war. A shadow passed across the window near the front door, momentarily blocking the moonlight. Savannah's breath caught. The floorboards creaked beneath her feet as she inched toward the door and held the pistol with trembling hands.

The front door handle rattled violently. Savannah's finger hovered over the trigger, her palms slick with sweat. As the rattling intensified, she realized with growing horror that the bar across the door was slowly, inexplicably, beginning to slide open of its own accord.

"Savannah?"

She fought the faint with adrenaline alone. The rattling stopped, and a familiar voice reached her through the side door. Savannah rushed through the room to the kitchen and lifted the bar from the door. She opened the door inward and nearly fell against Hayes, stopping herself by bolstering her arm against the doorframe.

"Hayes." She feared an attack on her heart and forced her breathing to slow. "How did you know?" Savannah asked between heavy breaths.

Whether the pounding of her own heartbeat or the shifting of logs on the fire awakened her, Savannah found herself still in the rocker, the wind howling beyond the secure doors and paned windows. Her skin tingled, and when she raised the back of her hand to her forehead, she wiped away a sheen of moisture.

Savannah's eyes darted around the room, seeking reassurance in the familiar surroundings. The fire crackled, casting dancing shadows on the walls, and the scent of pine from the logs lingered in the air. She exhaled slowly, willing her racing heart to calm.

"Only a dream," she whispered, her voice barely audible above the wind's mournful song.

Rising from the rocker, Savannah moved to the window, her stockinged feet padding softly across the wooden floor. She peered into the darkness, searching for any movement beyond the glass. The moon hung low in the sky, a pale orb partially obscured by scudding clouds and whisper soft snowflakes. Darkness stretched out before her, silvered by moonlight.

As her breathing steadied, Savannah's thoughts turned again to Hayes. Even in her dreams, he appeared as a source of comfort and strength. She closed her eyes, recalling the warmth of his presence, the steadiness of his voice. A bittersweet ache bloomed in her chest.

"Enough mourning for what might have been, Savannah." She adjusted the logs in the hearth to ensure none would shift and roll, then retreated to her small bedroom. A wrought iron double bed took up half the room and a clothes wardrobe stood against the wall opposite the single window. She'd left the curtains parted here as well, as she often did.

Tonight, she skirted the bed and drew the curtains to block out the night. Dream or not, she wanted as much barrier between herself and the darkness as possible. Twenty minutes later, ready for bed, she left a lamp burning low before pulling back the covers, sliding into bed, and pulling the quilts to just beneath her chin. Exhaustion won over fear, and she fell asleep minutes later.

Hayes stared through the window next to the bed and up at the same smattering of stars and silvery moon Savannah had. Only, he was not enjoying the same slumber. Despite the medicine Dr. Walker had given him, sleep remained elusive. Knowing Savannah slept nearby in the cabin behind the clinic did not help settle Hayes's thoughts.

He sat up in bed and opened *Great Expectations*. He'd read it once before, in 1864, after his captain loaned him a copy. Novels had been a welcome diversion on the battlefields, especially during long waiting periods of silence between battles.

The familiar words of Dickens's prose danced before Hayes's eyes, but his mind wandered, unable to focus on the tale of Pip and Estella. Instead, he reflected on his own great expectations. Now, in the quiet of this frontier town, with Savannah's gentle presence nearby, he felt the stirrings of something he had long ago abandoned—hope. He had finally, after all this time, found her.

Hayes closed the book with a sigh and testing his injured side, kept his arm close to his chest as he eased to the edge of the bed, dragging the thinner of two blankets from the bed and awkwardly draping it around his shoulders. The floorboards creaked beneath his stockinged feet as he stood and walked to the clinic's front room where the stove still gave off heat.

A light passed through a front window seconds before a key turned in the lock, and the front door opened. Dr. Taylor Walker hurried inside and closed the door quickly behind him. He hadn't done more than slip into pants, a wool coat, and boots over his union suit.

"I heard you moving around down here. Are you in pain?" Taylor hung the lantern on a hook.

Hayes shook his head and remained by the stove. "Not the kind of pain you can treat with medicine, I'm afraid. Can't sleep."

Taylor's brow furrowed with concern as he joined Hayes at the stove. "The medicine should have helped with that. Nightmares?"

"You figured out how to rid yourself of them?" At Taylor's raised brow, Hayes added, "Savannah mentioned you were a surgeon during the war."

"Ah." Taylor added two more small pieces of wood to the stove. "I've yet to meet a soldier who has fought back their nightmares, at least not entirely. Most of them fade with enough time. Is it nightmares plaguing you or Savannah?"

Hayes rubbed his hands together, wishing he'd covered himself with a heavier quilt. "No offense Doc, but I expect your obligation to keep confidences doesn't extend to non-medical concerns."

"Depends." Taylor walked to his cupboard and mixed more powder into a glass of water. "Drink this. Without sleep, your body won't heal, and moving around isn't helping."

Hayes accepted the glass but didn't drink.

"Unless you want to be laid up for weeks instead of days, drink it."

Feeling like a chastised adolescent, Hayes drank, then handed the glass back. "Does anyone ever say no to you?"

"Plenty." Taylor grinned. "The first time. Then most get wise. Do you want help getting back to bed?"

"I can manage."

"See that you do." Taylor started for the door. "If you need motivation to do what I say, at least until I remove your stitches, consider whether *not* listening is helping her." With those parting words, the doctor took up his lantern, exited the building, and locked the door.

Hayes waited until the lantern light passed by the

window before he returned to the back room. Whatever the doctor had given him this time seemed to work fast. Or his mind and body were finally in agreement. Whatever the case, once Hayes found a comfortable position on his back and pulled up the quilts, he closed his eyes. Blessedly, he slept.

When he awakened with the sun high, it was to soft humming, a sweet sound so faint he thought he might still be dreaming. With a clearer head and a little pain, Hayes slid out of bed. Washing and dressing proved challenging, and as much as he would have appreciated Savannah's help, he opted not to test temptation. He sat to tug on his boots, cursed softly at the sharp pain in his side, and stared at the door when a soft knock sounded from the other side.

"I'm decent."

Savannah entered, carrying fresh towels and sheets. Upon spying one boot tipped over on the floor, she set the linens on the bed's edge and kneeled on the rug in front of Hayes. "You could have said something." She picked up the boot and held it out. When he did not raise his foot, she tapped his knee.

Chuckling, Hayes accepted her help. Once the boot was on his foot, he stood and stomped his feet twice. "I've often thought if we'd only had women generals, the war would have ended in half the time."

"You give us too much credit." She tilted her head slightly to the right, releasing a tendril from the loose knot to curl over her brow. "You look better. Dr. Walker told me of your restlessness last night. Dr. Walker was called to the mine this morning, leaving you under my care. How are you?"

"Better."

She raised her brow and continued to watch him. Sunlight shined through the window, casting soft rays of light across the room and illuminating the lines of speculation on her face.

"All right. Better than yesterday."

Savannah accepted the revised response with a single nod. "The café has already delivered breakfast, though it is likely cooled now. I can warm it on the stove."

Hayes sought a clock but found none in the room. "What time is it?"

"Half-past nine when I last checked. How are your stitches? And keep in mind I will know if you lie."

"The soldiers in your care must have been terrified of you." Hayes shrugged as though testing his wound again. "It pulled some this morning."

"Most of the men claimed I was an angel, though I always suspected the morphine spoke for them." She started for the recovery room door. "Come along. We will eat once I ensure you have not ruined Dr. Walker's fine work."

Hayes followed Savannah into the front room and sat when she patted the examination table. The graceful movement of her hands drew his gaze as she prepared to examine his wound. The morning sunlight streaming through the window caught her chestnut hair, creating a warm halo around her face.

"You'll need to unbutton your shirt and union suit enough for me to view the wound area," Savannah instructed as she poured hot water from a kettle into a stoneware bowl.

Hayes complied, wincing slightly as the fabric dragged against the dressing covering the stitches. Savannah's fingers were cool against his skin as she scrutinized the threads. Her touch sent a shiver through him that had nothing to do with pain.

"You are fortunate," she murmured, her breath warm against his shoulder. "The wound isn't showing any signs of infection, and despite your exertions, the sutures are holding."

Hayes turned to face her, suddenly aware of how close they were standing. "I suspect that has more to do with my doctor and nurse than luck."

Savannah's cheeks flushed, and she ducked her head, busying herself with replacing the bandage. "You give me too much credit, though I assure you, Dr. Walker deserves the praise."

"Did you know him before you came out west?" He reached out to tilt her chin up. "Did you ever work in the field with him?"

Their eyes locked, and the world around them seemed to fade away for a moment. The warmth and compassion in Savannah's gaze drew Hayes in, and he felt a sense of satisfaction when he realized he had momentarily left her speechless. He grinned. "Savannah?"

"What? No." She stepped back and cleared her throat. Savannah kept her gaze averted as she cleaned and covered the wound. "You may redress now. No, I did not know Taylor before I moved here. Although, I had heard of him. I asked him once why a man of his skills came to this remote mountain valley to practice medicine when any hospital would have proudly accepted him."

"What did he say?"

Savannah crossed the floor to Dr. Walker's medicine shelves. Instead of mixing anything, she picked up a glass and carried it back. "He never said, and I haven't asked again. Dr. Walker prepared this for you before he left. He said it won't put you to sleep; it is to help with the pain."

Once Hayes drank it, Savannah motioned to the table where they'd eaten dinner the evening before. "It will not take long to warm the food."

True to her word, not ten minutes later, she set a plate of hotcakes, scrambled eggs, sausage, and applesauce in front of him. "I did not know your preference, so there is both maple syrup and molasses for the hotcakes. Dr. Walker said you are to eat everything, regardless of whether you are hungry or not."

"You're back to calling him Dr. Walker."

Savannah held a small spoon of applesauce to her mouth and ate it before answering. "Since your observation yesterday, I have had to make a conscious effort to think before calling him Taylor. It will take time. I sent word to Cooper McCord and asked him to visit the clinic today."

Hayes considered her as he cut a sausage in half. "My opinion about you offering help hasn't changed. It's too dangerous. I have no idea what Elijah has gotten himself into, and speculating makes my head pound because I switch between best- and worst-case scenarios." Hayes ate the sausage in two bites, then drizzled a little maple syrup on his hotcakes. "I don't want you to think I don't appreciate it. You saved my life, Savannah."

"Do you think you owe me something for saving your life?"

"No." He said it quickly enough to erase the faint frown lines around her mouth. "You would have done the same for anyone because it's who you are. I know my confession about coming here to find you was unexpected, and if you tell me now that I miscalculated—"

"I have not said so."

Hayes set his fork and knife on the edge of his plate. "All right, we'll get back to that later. I'll accept whatever help I can get to find my brother."

"But not from me." Savannah dabbed her mouth with the edge of a napkin.

"Promise your help will end with introductions, and I'll say no more about it."

Savannah rose. "Would you like tea? Dr. Walker—Taylor—dries various herbs and swears by their efficacy."

Hayes watched her straight back as she measured dried herbs into a teapot and poured hot water from the kettle into the pot. She never wasted a movement. "Savannah—"

The knock at the door annoyed Hayes even as he was grateful for the interruption. Savannah opened the door and welcomed in a tall man dressed like he'd been dog sledding. Hayes expected most women would find him handsome. When the man smiled warmly at Savannah, she returned it easily.

"Cooper. Thank you for coming so quickly."

Cooper McCord. Married. Once Hayes recalled that bit of information, he smiled at the newcomer.

"Hayes Munro, Cooper McCord, whom I told you about." She ushered Cooper inside to the stove, but the man remained near the door, seemingly unaffected by the frigid winter air.

Hayes stood and held out his hand, which Cooper accepted and shook. "Mr. Munro."

"Please, it's Hayes. Did Savannah mention why you've been invited here?"

Cooper's penetrating gaze scrutinized Hayes. "You're looking for someone." Cooper glanced at Savannah. "She left out the details."

"Have you ever heard of Elijah McCord?" Cooper asked Hayes, "You related to him?"

Hayes nodded. "My brother. You've heard the name."

"I have," Cooper said, "And I've met the man. The second week of September, I helped the territorial marshal and his deputies track a group of robbers from Butte into the wilderness about two hours east of here. They swiped the payroll from a mine. Your brother gave me their direction, or what he believed to be their next destination."

"He wasn't with the robbers?"

"Unconfirmed. He'd worked in the same mine for almost a month before the robbery. I suspect he was their inside man."

Hayes gripped the top rail of the chair until his knuckles turned white. He could find a dozen ways to blame himself, and not a single one excused or exonerated Elijah if he was indeed part of the outlaw group. "Did you find them?"

"Two weeks later in the opposite direction, and less than an hour from Whitcomb Springs. The mine here has been spared, mainly because it's harder to get to and the Whitcombs have kept the yield low the past year to temper temptation and work on reclamation plans."

Savannah asked, "Was Elijah among the men arrested?"

Cooper looked at Hayes when he answered. "He was not. I haven't heard Elijah McCord's name since, and the men they brought in never mentioned him."

Hayes slowly nodded. "Thank you." He held out his hand again and Cooper shook it. "If you hear anything, would you let me know?"

"I will." Cooper tucked his thumbs into his pockets.

"Savannah's note isn't the only reason I'm here. Our sheriff sent a wire, got held up by a winter storm over the western pass, and broke his leg. He'll be spending the next little while in Virginia City."

"And you're here to find out how I ended up here, shot, and now what you know about my brother, you're wondering if I'm hiding something."

Cooper smiled. "I did. This conversation dissuaded me from those thoughts. However, Taylor filled me on what you told him about riding across the camp. You were shot just north of town, and that concerns us all. We're forming a search party, and we'll head out as soon as you and I finish here."

Hayes stepped forward. "I'll ride with you."

"No, you will not." Savannah stepped between the two men. "You are in no condition to ride, at least for a few more days. If you won't listen to me, I assure you, Cooper will tie you to the bed and you can deal with Dr. Walker."

Hayes raised his brow in question to Cooper, who merely nodded and smiled again.

"I won't sit here idle while others risk their lives."

Savannah opened her mouth to protest, but Hayes silenced her with a determined look. She didn't remain silent for long. "If you can pull yourself onto the back of a horse without pulling the stitches and opening your wound, then by all means." Savannah swept her hand out and toward the door.

Cooper stopped a smile from forming. "I promise to let you know if we come across any sign of your horse or gear. Do you remember how far you rode before you fell off?"

Hayes shook his head. "The sun didn't move much. It felt longer, but I'd guess only fifteen or twenty minutes."

"Anyone who might have been out in this cold overnight

won't be alive. We'll find them if they're out there." Cooper said goodbye to Savannah and left them alone in the clinic.

Hayes's eyes softened as he gazed at Savannah, her concern for him evident in the furrow of her brow. He took a tentative step forward. "Savannah, I appreciate your care more than you know. But I can't just sit here while others are in danger."

She moved closer, within six inches of him. "And I can't bear the thought of you risking your life when you're not fully healed. I overstepped, but I won't apologize."

Hayes chuckled, his thumb tracing the curve of her cheekbone. "I'd be sorry if you did. I meant what I said, though. While others find put themselves at risk going after the men—"

"Your brother?"

He nodded slowly and dropped his hand to her shoulder. "It's possible, even as I hope it's not. Elijah was always a good kid, carefree. I have to believe if he has somehow involved himself with dangerous men that it's not of his choosing."

Savannah skimmed a delicate touch over Hayes's hand. "You can trust Cooper and the other men in town. I've learned that people who are trouble are quickly run out of Whitcomb Springs. The Whitcombs are tolerant people so long as everyone treats everyone honestly and fairly."

Hayes stepped away from her and walked to the window. Ice crystals had formed around the sill, and if he got too close, his breath fogged the glass. "Does Whitcomb Springs have a bank?"

Savannah took a moment to adjust her thoughts to the subject shift. "Not a traditional bank that makes loans and invests money. This past summer, the town finished building the only brick structure, and it serves as the town's bank. It's used to hold payroll for the mine and lumber mill, and it's where they disperse payroll. Many of the townspeople keep their money in the safe there for security, but it all stays in town."

"Enough money to interest a group of robbers?"

"I imagine so, though less in winter. The mine does not produce as much once the heavy snow falls, and the timber operation continues so long as weather permits, but fewer men are working."

Hayes turned and leaned against the window frame. "You've settled in here."

Savannah nodded and smiled. "People here are friendly and eager to strike up conversations. This is my first winter. If you stay long enough—at least a week—you'll learn a good deal more about the town."

He planned to stay, and much longer than a week. Of Savannah, he asked, "When do they disperse payroll?"

"Mondays, in the morning."

"Is it Wednesday now?"

"Thursday." Like a good nurse, Savannah automatically pressed the back of her hand to his forehead. "No fever. What is the last day you remember?"

Hayes grabbed her hand, kissed her knuckles, and tucked it against his chest. "Monday, or I thought it was Monday when I was shot. You found me Tuesday morning?"

Savannah nodded. "It's easy to lose track of time out here. What were you doing right before you heard the shot?"

Hayes gazed out the window again and saw a group of men ride north of town toward the meadow where Savannah had found him. He took her hand and walked back to the cushioned chair, sat her down in it, and took a seat in the wooden chair she'd moved over earlier. "Admiring the thick clouds touched with gray hovering over the mountain peaks and the mist settling over the valley. There was elk, I think, a small herd, in the distance. My binoculars went over a cliff the day before when I was watching an eagle. The scent of pine filled the air; I'd never smelled anything so fresh. The air is so much heavier in the Carolinas."

"I saw the smoke and rode toward it, found the camp." He leaned back in the chair. "Then there was the familiar pinch and burning sensation. Like I told Cooper, I rode for a ways, then blacked out—couldn't have been for long because my clothes weren't too wet yet from lying in the snow—and when I came to, my horse was gone. I gathered my bearings enough to head in my original direction."

"Whitcomb Springs."

Hayes nodded and rubbed the back of his head. "I spent so long looking over my shoulder, barely sleeping for worry about the next battle or the blade of a desperate man. When I finally reached this valley, everything inside of me stopped, and for a moment, I believed peace existed."

Savannah leaned forward and gripped his hands, which had tightened into fists. "Peace does exist here, Hayes. Despite your present condition leading you to believe otherwise, yours is the first bullet wound I've helped treat since arriving here."

"Peace has been a stranger to me for so long; I'm not sure I'd recognize it if it walked right up and shook my hand."

Savannah's lips curved into a gentle smile. "Perhaps it's not about recognizing peace but allowing yourself to feel it. To breathe it in, like the crisp mountain air." She released his hands and stood. "I think Dr. Walker would recommend a short walk in fresh air."

Hayes also stood, and giving in to the impulse, leaned down and kissed her cheek. He appreciated the faint rosy color infusing her fair skin. "I'd like that." The peace he'd briefly felt and hoped for as he stood on the rough-textured rocks overlooking the valley slowly returned.

CHAPTER FOUR

Savannah cast an occasional glance toward Hayes and noticed his eyes close for a few seconds as he lifted his face toward the sunrays peeking through heavy white clouds. She kept her arm linked with his so his step never faltered, and neither did hers. Other times she caught him scanning the horizon or glancing at her profile, sometimes with a smile and sometimes with a look of contemplation.

Although it offered no warmth, the sun teased more people from their homes. Mothers watched after their children as they walked from one place to the next, sometimes stopping to visit with another passerby. With school closed until after Christmas, older children ventured out to play in the snow or help their parents with tasks.

It had taken little time for Savannah to feel welcome and at home, and now she couldn't imagine ever leaving. Hayes's confession about journeying from South Carolina to this faraway territory to find her continued to fill her thoughts. One woman with a blanket-bundled toddler on her hip waved to them before she hurried into the general store. Two men hauling a large wooden cart of cut wood tipped their hats with a smile and continued into the heart of town.

Savannah and Hayes walked in silence from the clinic to where the meadow met Daniel and Evelyn Whitcomb's house. She smiled when Hayes faced her and adjusted her thick, green-knit scarf so it covered more of her neck.

"Does everyone live in town?"

Savannah shook her head as her gaze shifted to the Whitcomb house. "Most do, though there are a few farms farther out. I've been told the expense of getting supplies here is a deterrent for significant growth, and I believe the townspeople prefer it that way. The Whitcombs made most of what you see possible. There were two other original founders. One passed his first winter, and the other did not return after the war. The Whitcomb Timber and Mining Company keeps most families solvent, and the other smaller businesses keep them content."

"Is there a lumber mill?"

Curious at the direction of his questions, Savannah said, "There is a small sawmill, though Cooper mentioned to Dr. Walker that there is hope to expand it if the Whitcombs can find a partner they can trust." She tapped his shoulder and drew his full attention. "Are your questions posed merely out of interest?"

"Merely?" Hayes shook his head. "There is nothing simple about my interest." He ran a gloved thumb over her mouth. "We should get back. It's colder than I realized until we stopped." He linked her arm through his once more, and they made their way leisurely back to the clinic, walking back over their prints in the snow. "Do you know of any empty houses for rent or purchase?"

Surprised, she almost tripped on her own booted feet. Hayes held her steady. "You plan to stay on here, then?"

Hayes smiled. "Once I heal enough to satisfy Dr. Walker, I will need to find other accommodations. Taylor mentioned a small hotel, which could work temporarily."

She did not recall his being so hard to read in their youth. "Yes, the hotel has room available. I ask in case we ever have more patients than we can accommodate here. Bachelors who stay over the winter fill the boardinghouse."

They reached the clinic, and the door opened to them before Hayes's reached for the handle. Dr. Walker, with dark circles under his eyes and a day's growth of beard, ushered them inside.

"I was about to go out and look for you when I saw you walking back." He poured hot water into two stoneware mugs and put them on the table. "Tea. Drink it. Savannah prefers it, and you would do well to avoid coffee for another day."

"Dr. Walker believes the stimulants in coffee impede initial healing." Savannah smiled as she unwound her scarf and allowed Hayes to help her remove her wool cloak before she hung it on the hook and eased her chilled hands from their gloves. Hayes had his coat half off by the time she reached for it.

"Months at my side and I can rarely get her to call me Taylor." He pointed to Hayes. "This one took to it just fine. Yes, my thinking does not always set well with the men in town, though most at least let me think they follow my directives." Taylor rubbed a hand over his face, hair, and the back of his neck.

Savannah's smile faltered. "What happened?"

"Rosie Smith lost her baby this morning. There was nothing to be done by the time they asked for me. Lyle

Jack's son left before you arrived. Lyle broke his arm and refused to leave his farm, so I need to return to set and properly immobilize it."

"I will go with you."

Taylor shook his head at Savannah. "You haven't had the joy of treating Lyle yet, and we will keep it that way. He does not approve of nurses and will not have one near him, or so said his wife the last time I was out there treating their youngest for colic." Taylor apologized with a shrug. "Something to do with treatment for Lyle's pneumonia during the war." He glanced longingly at the woodstove before gathering his outer clothing and reaching for his medical bag. "Hayes, no more walking outside today. I'll check the wound when I return, and you should be well enough to move to the hotel tomorrow."

Without another word, Taylor left the clinic with a loud thud when he closed the door.

"When anyone ended up in a field hospital during the war, we always hoped for a doctor like him. There weren't many." Hayes sniffed the tea before sipping. "He'll put himself in an early grave going at that pace."

"He will not slow down, even when he admonishes me—and others—to do the same." Savannah did not need to sniff the tea before drinking generously. "I have not had so much as a cold since I started drinking his concoctions."

Hayes drew her back to their earlier conversation with his next question. "About available long-term lodging around here . . ."

She drank another generous helping of the tea and wrapped her hands around the warm mug. "If a falling star shoots across the sky tonight, I will wish only to become wise to your thoughts, for you, Hayes Munro, are miserly with your words."

He grinned in answer. "You would not wish to know *all* my thoughts, Savannah Quinn." Hayes sipped again at the tea. "Miserly, huh? We have come full circle to my reason for coming to Whitcomb Springs. To find you." He paused long enough to make sure she understood. "Is this home now, or is home back in Charleston?"

Savannah considered this place her home now, yet a thought scrambled to the forefront: Home is with Hayes. She did not give voice to the thought, for it had once been an unfulfilled dream. "This is a good place." It seems Hayes was not the only word miser. "What did you do after the war? Did you also join your uncle to learn medicine?"

Hayes considered her for a moment before answering. "I had too much respect for the doctors and nurses who fought so hard to save wounded soldiers, so no, medicine was never my calling. My father sent me to Yale, wanting me to learn business. I never saw the point of it. I only wanted to work with horses. There wasn't a reason to stay, so I went."

Savannah fondly remembered him teaching her how to ride. Of course, that was before her father realized Hayes's interest in her. "Yale is the one in Connecticut, isn't it?"

Hayes nodded. "During that time, my father invested in a shipping company, sold the textile store, and planned for me to join him in business."

"You didn't?"

"Not for long. His heart gave out. After the funeral, my mother wanted to live closer to her brother and his family. Elijah came west, and I heard you did as well." Hayes stood, checked the water in the kettle on the stove, and warmed both their tea mugs before returning the kettle. He remained standing, though. "It took some time to sell my father's interest in the shipping company, sell the house, and secure my mother's living."

Savannah had to wait for the catch in her chest to clear before asking, "Then you are not returning?"

"Not unless you ask me to."

The clinic door opened in a rush, and Cooper, red-faced with his hat covered in fresh snow, asked, "Where's the Doc?"

Savannah nearly toppled her chair in her haste to stand. "He went to the Jack's farm. Who is hurt?"

Cooper stepped aside as three men carried in a younger man Savannah had never seen before. "Don't know who, but he's in a bad way."

Savannah waited until they'd laid the injured man on the examination table and carefully lowered the blanket they had laid over his body, from head to ankle. His scuffed boots protruded from beneath the scratchy wool. "Where did you find him?"

"At the base of Whisper Ridge." Cooper removed his glove and rubbed his hands together. "He's not Elijah," Cooper added before Hayes asked.

Savannah asked without taking her eyes off the patient, "Cooper, help me remove his coat." Once the man was down to his union suit, Savannah pressed against his chest, legs, and arms. "No blood."

Cooper told the men who'd brought the injured one inside that he'd catch up with them soon. Once they'd left, he said to Savannah and Hayes, "No blood, or wounds that might cause them, so he didn't fall. The camp you came across, Hayes, was abandoned, the embers long since out and covered with a fresh layer of snow."

He jerked his head away from the table, asking Cooper

to follow him. They stepped three feet away, giving Savannah enough room to work.

Hayes asked, "What about a horse?"

Cooper nodded. "A mare—gray quarter horse. She's healthy, though wild-spirited when we tried to grab her reins. She kicked Pete—he works timber during the summer months—and seemed like she planned to keep going before my chestnut gelding calmed her. No saddlebags, and we found no other gear."

"That sounds like the horse I bought off the farmer." Hayes glanced at the man. "Do you think this man was with the ones who shot me?"

"Maybe, though not one I recognize, and he doesn't match any of the descriptions we've received so far, which doesn't mean much."

Hayes cursed his injury and rubbed his hand stiffly below the sutured wound. He itched to ride out to see for himself, though according to Savannah, no one knew the land better than Cooper. Tomorrow he could leave the clinic, and he'd suffered worse injuries. "What else?"

"Signs of three other riders before the new snow started falling. Night comes early this time of year, and I couldn't risk us staying out later once the snow started falling again. The flakes are coming down thick. It takes only a few minutes in the weather before someone can lose their way. If the other riders haven't found shelter by now, we'll discover more bodies come spring."

Hayes glanced out the window and saw that the filtered sunlight and bright clouds had given way to a mass of gray that blocked the once-visible smatterings of blue sky. Snow drifted from those gray clouds in a thick and steady curtain of white. "Do you think they're foolish enough to be caught in the elements?"

"Not if it's the group the marshal and every other lawman in the area is hunting. They're smart," Copper said. "If it clears, I'll go back out tomorrow."

"If it clears, I'll go with you. I need to find Elijah." Hayes studied Savannah's curved back as she bent over the man. She'd cut his pant legs up to the lower part of his thighs, and his union suit splayed open.

"Hayes."

He was by Savannah's side in two steps. The man's pale chest rose and fell with quick and unsteady breaths. Just below the left side of his ribs, a long gash parted the skin to his lower belly. A bandanna soaked in blood lay in a bowl on the examination table. He prayed it wasn't as bad as it looked, if only to be able to question him. "Will he live?"

Savannah never took her eyes off the man as she carefully used tweezers to remove loose threads before covering the wound with clean cloths. "I need Dr. Walker." She raised her head then to look out the window, except there was nothing to see beyond the snow.

"I can fetch him," Cooper said, "but it might take some time. Can you keep him alive until then?"

Savannah shook her head. "Dr. Walker may well end up with two patients if you ride out in this, and your wife would forgive none of us." She looked at Hayes, who still stood by her elbow. Her eyes steadied on him. "You said you have an uncle who is a doctor. Did you ever study with him?"

"The summer after you left." Hayes thought his mind and eyes had become benumbed to the sight of injury and death. The worst of all he'd ever seen returned and roiled his stomach. "It's been a long time."

She nudged him with her elbow to gain his attention. "I

have no choice but to help this man. You do. I will understand, considering he might have—"

Hayes circled the table. "What do you need?"

They worked together, with Savannah instructing Cooper on what to gather from different places in the clinic and explaining what she needed mixed from the herbs in Dr. Walker's medicinal stores. Her voice, with the faintest hint of their once-home in South Carolina, was firm yet soft, gentle yet authoritative. Hayes imagined her in a field hospital, directing doctors and patients, and imagined her every bit as effective as Generals Lee or Grant in getting the men to follow orders.

After a thorough hand washing, her long fingers probed and cleaned the wound, and when the man twitched, she instructed Cooper on how to administer chloroform carefully by pouring three drops on a clean cloth and holding it over the nose and mouth. "I have never been comfortable determining how much to use or for how long." She spoke more to herself than the men. "That should be enough," she said to Cooper. "Dr. Walker uses it sparingly because he has seen men die from improper use, though some doctors in the field hospitals were wont to use it liberally."

Savannah secured the last stitch before cleaning around the wound with the saline solution Cooper brought to the table. "Infection is always the biggest worry. Dr. Walker—Taylor—would know what to do next, and I cannot say I did everything correctly. I have observed and assisted in several surgeries, but . . ." Savannah gazed at Hayes. "It is possible—"

"Don't." Hayes wiped blood from his fingers. "You've done what you could, and from where I stood, no one else could have done better. Taylor will tell you the same thing. The wound . . ."

Savannah nodded, for they both understood the chances of recovering from a wound like this man's, and that was from only what they could see. "There could be more wrong on the inside. We need to check the rest of him." She cleaned her hands again before raising a pair of scissors. "Cooper, please remove his boots. Carefully. We cannot risk jostling his body too much."

Cooper did. Hayes reached across the body and took the scissors from her hand. "I'll cut the pants off and check for any other injury."

Savannah thanked him as she gathered the soiled cloths and instruments she'd used and carried them over to the cleaning table, where a bucket of water waited for washing. Cooper carried a kettle of boiled water from the stove to the table where she worked and poured half into a large basin. At her bidding, he filled another bowl with the remaining water, and into which she dropped the soiled cloths.

When she returned to the examination table, Hayes had covered the man with a wool blanket. The pants, now cut in pieces, lay on the small wooden chair by the front door with the boots.

"I found no injuries on his legs."

Savannah nodded. "His breathing is still unsteady."

Hayes circled the table once more and turned her to face him. "You did all you could." Not caring that she still wore the apron with specks of blood, he brought her close and held her.

Cooper met Hayes's gaze over Savannah's head. Cooper pointed at the front door and held up both hands with all ten fingers splayed. At Hayes's nod, Cooper slipped into his coat and gloves and quietly left, the door barely making a sound as he opened and closed it. The wind had mellowed, so all that entered was cold and a few snowflakes.

Savannah remained in Hayes's embrace, content for the moment to share the weight of their bodies and burdens. She recalled every detail of the day she was forced to say goodbye to him. He'd been working with the horses and had yet to clean up before the picnic he'd planned for them that afternoon.

He was taller now, his chest thicker, his arms stronger. When he rested his cheek against her hair, she closed her eyes and wished away all the years in between. "I still have much to do."

Hayes leaned back a little and lifted her chin again. "There are two of us here, and I'm not going anywhere."

She longed to ask him if he meant right now or forever. Given their proximity to a grievously wounded man, and her fractured nerves, she held her question for a better time. With regret, she stepped back and smoothed the front of her apron. "I need to change my apron, and you could use a clean shirt. Dr. Walker keeps a few extra shirts in the hall bureau in case someone needs them. There should be one that will fit you. When the weather clears, we can go to the general store and order you new clothes."

Hayes nodded and left her to go into the hall. She heard the bureau door open, then close a few seconds later. Savannah followed his movements by the sound of his quiet tread on the board floors.

Savannah hadn't thought to ask a question before that now occupied her mind, so when she removed her soiled apron, she walked to the room Hayes was temporarily using. She had not expected the door to be open or for

Hayes's back to be bare. What she saw caused her to suck in a deep breath.

He must have heard her, for he paused in lifting the first shirt over his head. After an indeterminable amount of time, at least in Savannah's mind, Hayes lowered the thick white cotton shirt over his head before picking up a dark-green, flannel shirt that buttoned up the front.

Hayes turned as he slipped his arms into the sleeves. "They healed long ago."

Savannah tried and failed to erase the image from her mind. Four randomly placed narrow burns, between three and four inches, scarred the center of his back and his left shoulder blade. For the first time in her memory, Savannah longed for revenge.

"Who did that to you?"

Hayes raised his brow at the vehemence in her voice while he buttoned the shirt. "A soldier whose name I never knew. They don't hurt, Savannah."

"But they did." *Excruciatingly*, she silently added. "Did a fire poker make those marks?"

Hayes said nothing at first. To give himself a little more time, he lifted the shirts and checked his recent wound. Dr. Walker's stitches held, and there was no sign of bleeding, swelling, or infection. "Where did Taylor study medicine?"

"Harvard, and do not change the subject, Hayes Munro."

"I never gave much credence to those fancy schools, especially while I was attending one, but I've changed my mind. They taught him well." Hayes tucked the first shirt into his pants and let the second hang over the sides. "Yes." He held out his hand for her to take. When she did, he pulled her forward, and they both sat on the bed's edge. "I told you that they took me prisoner after Vicksburg. My father understood why I had joined the Union instead of the Confederacy. My mother didn't forgive me, and Elijah called me a fool. I don't regret my decision, but it split my family, and I wasn't the only southerner in our town to join the North. General Grant paroled most of the Confederate soldiers after Vicksburg, and yet, hatred ran deep in the blood, hearts, and earth of the South.

"Five soldiers took me and one other prisoner, though we never made it to a prison. We stopped at a farm one night and they decided to pass the time. The farm had a forge." Hayes did not have to explain what happened next, for she had already seen it on his back. "The soldiers found three bottles of wine in a root cellar after they finished with my back and my comrade's arms." He shrugged. "They drank, slept, and we escaped."

Savannah cupped his face against her palm, her smooth skin to his unshaven. "I wish I had been there."

Hayes laughed. He didn't know where it came from, but it felt good, and seeing the curve of her lips, she knew he was not making light of her statement. Hayes turned his face toward her palm, kissed the soft skin, and then took her hand. "For all the right reasons, I am very glad you weren't there. I wish you hadn't been there for any of it."

Savannah sobered. "I needed to do my part, even if at first I became a nurse, hoping to see you. However, in the hospitals where I worked, we rarely treated Union soldiers."

"Scars heal, some more quickly than others." Savannah kissed his hand, a faint touch of her mouth to his skin meant to comfort. It wasn't enough.

She always wondered what the great mined who coined the phrase, "The eyes are the window to your soul," meant, until she looked into Hayes's eyes. A shadow of sorrow hovered beneath the warmth and love radiating, she knew, for her. Her fingertips trailed lightly over his jaw before she scooted closer. Hayes leaned into her touch, his gaze softening as she drew nearer. She could feel the warmth of his breath on her skin and held hers a moment before she pressed her lips to his.

The kiss remained gentle, a remembering of a time long ago when two young people, full of hope and dreams, imagined a future together. When they finally parted, she rested her forehead against his, extending the moment.

"All these years, I've never stopped thinking about you." Hayes wanted to pull her in again for another kiss. However, he sensed she needed to maintain control this time, and to make the choice of how quickly they moved forward. Instead, he rubbed the back of her hand when he said, "It's easy enough to forget the physical scars I can't see. Are the ones you can see something you can live with?" He knew what he was asking, and from the hitch in Savannah's breath, he knew she knew it, too.

With a serene expression, she nodded, her eyes reflecting the love she must surely see in his. "Yes, Hayes Munro, I can live with them, and everything else."

CHAPTER FIVE

"Did you travel here with only what you carried on the horse?"

Two more days had passed, most of that time inside the clinic as Hayes waited for the storm to let up. He'd known cold, or thought he had. The intensity of the cold in this part of the country caused him to check if ice crystals had formed on his skin. Savannah bundled herself in enough clothes to keep her warm, and though she occasionally tugged her scarf higher or her woolen hat lower, she seemed more impervious to the frigidness than Hayes.

He peered at her, smiling at how she sidled closer to him the moment they stepped outside and stood on the general store's covered porch. "I wanted to travel light and planned to send for the rest of my things once I'd found you."

Hayes appreciated the way her rosy cheeks brightened whenever he brought up why he'd come so far. Several years and a lot of living separated the sweet, first bloom of love with who they'd become. There was time to know each other again, to build on the foundation they'd once started.

No one else was around, wisely choosing to remain indoors unless necessity drove them outside. "I've started a letter home many times now, but I don't know what to tell our mother. She was devastated when Elijah left home. Until the weather clears, I can't go out and look for him."

Sunlight reflected off the snow, nearly blinding him when they stepped off the porch and onto the snow-covered road. Only a narrow section, enough room for a single wagon or sleigh to drive through, had been plowed so far, and paths cleared to homes and businesses.

"I saw them come through here with a horse-drawn plow. I'd never seen anything like it."

Savannah joined Hayes in stepping around a snow pile as high as her waist. "In Vermont, they used snow rollers. A team of four horses or sometimes oxen pulled a giant wheel along the roads to flatten the snow so sleighs and wagons with runners could move along the surface. I expect far too much snow falls here."

She didn't want to return to the clinic just now. Though frigid beneath the expansive blue sky, without a single cloud in sight to constrict the sun from casting off the snow and ice, Savannah wanted to fill her lungs with fresh air and feel the cold air against her face.

"You love it."

She smiled and nodded, somehow knowing what he meant. "No matter how often injury, illness, or even death insinuates itself into my life, nature reminds me how *alive* the world remains. When I don't watch where I'm walking and my boot sinks into mud, enveloping my shoe, when chirping birds awaken me from a deep sleep, when I help chase away an adventurous rabbit from Evelyn's vegetable garden, or even when the frosty air stings my face and I long for a warm hearth and cup of rich, hot chocolate. I welcome the minor annoyances because I know each living moment is a precious gift—a gift far too many men and women lose sight of while still in the blush of youth."

Savannah inhaled the cold to the full capacity of her lungs, held it, then released it warmly back into the air. When they stopped near the meadow's edge, close to a giant pine tree, Hayes turned her to face him. She lifted her face and her smile faltered at the intensity of his gaze. "I assure you, I am not afflicted with naivete or false hope. I simply—"

Hayes pressed a gloved finger to her lips. "I envy you the peace you've discovered in this place."

She grasped his hand and held it over her heart. "It is not only this place, Hayes. Yes, the people here, the beauty of the mountains, the scents of earth, pine, and wildflowers in the summer, the streams gurgling in the spring, they all helped facilitate my return to hope after losing so much. You, Hayes Munro, brought hope to full bloom. I thought you were gone forever."

Hayes cupped her face with both his hands. "Savannah—"

"Hayes."

The intrusion shattered the quiet spell between them. Hayes stiffened, and he brought her closer to him, covering her shoulders with his arms and blocking her from potential harm. An instinct she appreciated.

"What is wrong?"

Instead of answering her, Hayes stared into the face of a man, who, with a shave and haircut, would look like Hayes, eight years younger. "Elijah."

Of the few people venturing outdoors, none paid them

much attention. "What have you got yourself involved with, Elijah?"

Elijah gave his brother a half smile and shifted his attention. "Are you going to introduce us?"

"She already knows who you are, and you'll get her name after you answer my question."

Savannah's hand rested softly on Hayes's arm. "It is cold, and the road is no place for this conversation. We have no patients at the clinic, and you can be assured privacy."

Elijah said nothing, waiting for his brother. Hayes finally nodded, settled his arm around Savannah's waist, and told his brother to walk ahead of them.

Once indoors, no one had removed their hats or coats before Elijah said, "I need to talk to the sheriff."

"He is not here." Savannah unwound her green knitted scarf. "Taylor should be upstairs resting, so please keep your voices down, if you choose to shout." She removed her wool hat and cloak and hung both on a peg.

Hayes stopped his brother from walking farther into the warmer space. "I have imagined a dozen scenarios and even more possible conversations when I finally found you. Right now, I just want to flog you for what you have put Mother through."

Elijah held up his gloved hands. Only when Hayes stepped back a foot did he lower them. "You'd be justified, and it would be a fitting punishment, especially if Ma were standing judgment. If you'll let me explain?"

Hayes studied his brother for half a minute before nodding. "Savannah Quinn, this is my younger brother, Elijah McCord."

Elijah's head snapped back to Hayes and his smile waned. He silently mouthed, *Savannah?*

"Yes." Hayes put an end to any further inquiry. "Your

turn. Explain, because as far as some folks are concerned, you're part of an outlaw gang robbing mines between Butte and Cheyenne, and who knows what else."

Elijah remained silent, though he cast a furtive glance at Savannah.

Hayes leaned against a table between his brother and where Savannah was at the stove. "Whatever you say to me can be said in front of her."

"All right." Elijah removed his gloves and shoved them in his coat pocket. He took off his hat and held it in front of him. "With the sheriff gone, who passes for the law around here?"

Cooper entered the room from the hallway, his boots barely making a sound. "I can hear whatever you have to say."

Hayes's heavy sigh hung in the air before he waved a hand toward his brother. "Cooper McCord, I believe you've met my brother."

Elijah's eyes narrowed. "We've met."

"And now we meet again." Cooper leaned against the doorframe. "I'm also one of the men looking for you, so tell me now why I shouldn't lock you up until the territorial marshal can get here?"

Elijah's eyes shifted to his brother. Hayes nodded. "Because I'm not who you want, though God knows I don't deserve forgiveness for what I have done in the name of justice."

The men thanked Savannah as she passed mugs of coffee to them. When most women would have left them to their conversation, she remained, taking a seat near the stove with a cup of tea.

"There are four of them. Wayne Devlin and his brother Maurice, Percy Glass, and Roscoe Koch." Elijah's eyes shuttered. "There was a fifth, and I'm sorry to say I didn't stop Maurice when he sliced him up and left him for dead."

"He's dead now."

Three heads turned and three pairs of eyes focused on Cooper. Only Savannah moved. "When?"

"While you were out." Cooper held up a hand. "You couldn't have done anything, and neither could the doc. The man never woke up."

"Pete Chase was his name." Elijah drank deeply of the coffee, then coughed into his fist. "I need to explain."

Cooper said, "Why I don't tell you what I suspect, and you tell me yes or no?"

Elijah wiped his mouth and nodded.

"This group robbed the mine outside Virginia City."

Elijah nodded.

"They stole two horses and killed a farmer and his wife two miles outside Virginia City, then a week later slaughtered a small Crow hunting party on the Bozeman Trail."

Startlement reflected in Elijah's eyes. "I wasn't with them that day, but I suspected."

"They shot your brother when he came upon their camp."

This time Elijah looked at Hayes. "I caught up to them two days ago."

Hayes straightened and stepped toward his brother. "Where were you during the time you were separated from them?"

"Scouting."

Hayes swore, then grabbed a fist full of Elijah's wool shirt. "Scouting where?"

Elijah stood two inches shorter than his brother and

wasn't as broad through the chest and shoulders. To his credit, he didn't try to pull away. "Here."

"The Whitcomb mine?" Cooper asked.

"Yes, and the bank."

Hayes released his brother and shoved him away. "Where are they now? Still close?"

Elijah nodded. "One more job, then south."

"Tell me, brother, why have you come forward now?"

"I never intended for any of this to get so out of hand, Hayes." Elijah tossed his hat on a chair by the door and stepped back toward his brother. "The Devlin brothers tried to recruit me in Virginia City. At first, I told them I wasn't interested. That same night, the owner of one of the mines who was victim to the gang's thieving asked me to reconsider. He hired me to join the Devlins and see if I could find the money."

Cooper pushed away from the doorway, crossed the room, and pointed over his shoulder. "Did you recruit the dead man back there?"

"Yes, off a farm outside Butte."

"Who else knows about your arrangement with the mine owner?" Cooper asked.

With widened eyes, Elijah looked straight at Cooper. "Marshal Pinney. Didn't you know?"

Cooper didn't answer Elijah's question. "I'll ask Taylor to come down and confirm the death, then I'll send men to get him out of here for you, Savannah." Cooper reached for the front door handle. "I have to speak with Daniel Whitcomb about securing the mine before we go after the men."

"Wait." Hayes stepped toward him. "Can you find those men in this weather?"

Cooper pointed at Elijah. "We can because he's going to help us."

Elijah put his gloves back on and picked up his fallen hat. Before he left with Cooper, he said to his brother, "I'll make it all right again, Hayes. I promise."

Once alone, Savannah closed the distance between her and Hayes. As she stepped into his embrace, a faint scent of lavender wafted from her hair. Hayes's arms encircled her, their warmth shared. He appreciated how she fit perfectly against him, her head nestled just at the right height for him to rest his cheek against her soft hair, its silky strands brushing against his face.

He didn't want harsh realities to invade this precious moment, to draw his thoughts away from her. One day, maybe two and he would send word home. Even a telegram would not reach his mother before then, and regardless of the consequences his brother might face later, Elijah deserved a chance to make things right.

Savannah pulled back a little, her fingers grazing his cheek. "Taylor will no doubt be down momentarily." As she spoke, Hayes lifted her chin. Their lips met in a tender kiss, the sensation of their connection overwhelming her with a mix of love and longing.

Taylor indeed interrupted them not a minute later. "Apologies."

Hayes offered him a faint smile. "It's not a day for those." He brushed a kiss on Savannah's cheek. "I'm going to see about a room at the hotel. I won't be long."

Savannah watched him leave as Taylor left her alone. He spent less than five minutes in the back room, and when he returned, Savannah saw in his countenance what she had seen many times before—defeat. No matter how many lives one saved or lost, the losses somehow etched deeper into the soul. Even the undeserving ones.

Taylor passed by her to put the kettle on the woodstove. "You should rest, Savannah. Get away from here for at least a day. There are no patients now and everything else can keep." Taylor mixed herbs for tea and leaned against the scarred worktable, waiting for the water to boil. "Cooper told me enough to make me think we'll have more work soon enough."

She raised an eyebrow and crossed her arms over her chest. "And you will be no good to anyone in this town if you don't pace yourself. I understand your passion for your work, and you might even feel it's your obligation to be available to anyone who might need doctoring, but I have not seen you push yourself this much before."

Steam rose from the kettle, and Taylor poured the boiling water into two mugs. The rich, herbal aroma filled the small clinic as he passed her a mug. "I get more sleep now than I ever did during the war." He closed his eyes and drank deeply. "We're nearing two years of peace, except the killing of one another never seems to end."

"One could hope all the ailments, injuries, and misfortunes leave us alone, at least through Christmas."

Taylor smiled when he looked at her. "Have you celebrated Christmas yet, like before the war?"

Memories of Christmases past flitted through her mind, conjuring images she'd safely stored away: a fresh-cut tree delivered to the house in Charleston, or chopped down by her father in Vermont, left bare except for ribbons; the scent of spices and dried fruits baked into pies, cakes, and breads wafting from the kitchen; her mother's long fingers playing over ivory keys as they sang, "Silent Night," or a more robust rendering of "Joy to the World."

"No, not like before. In the years between . . ." Her voice trailed off, and she looked down at her tea, swirling the hot liquid around in her cup. More memories flooded back to her mind, memories of happier times before everything changed. She longed for that happiness again, the kind that made her heart sing and her soul light up. "I very much want to find that joy again."

Taylor drained his cup, set it in the washbasin, and crossed the room to her. "From what I've observed so far between you and Hayes, I'd say you'll have joy again soon." Surprising her, Taylor wrapped his arms around her in a gentle hug. When he pulled back, he was grinning, a grin the likes Savannah had not seen on him in months. "If he doesn't, he'll have to deal with me."

She laughed. "You are always so good to me, Taylor."

He softly chucked her on the chin. "That's what brothers do, Savannah." With a heavy sigh, he looked toward the hall. "Now, I'm going to get the body ready. When I come out here, you'd better be gone. Go home and sleep, visit with Evelyn and Abigail, or go for one of your long walks in the cold. Just be sure to get away from here for at least the rest of today. Do that for me?"

Asked in such a way, refusing would have been churlish. She was not in an ornery mood as her thoughts shifted to the man who occupied most of her thoughts these days. "Is Hayes well enough to ride with Cooper? We both know he will not sit by this time and wait."

Taylor stopped in the hallway. Dark circles marred the skin beneath his eyes, and he appeared to have lost a few pounds. "Hayes is strong and his wound is healing. He'll survive whatever he comes up against—for you." He disappeared into the hall, leaving Savannah alone with her thoughts.

Gripping her tea mug, she made her way toward the window, where the scene outside unfolded like a winter fairy tale. Snowflakes, gentle and ethereal, danced from the darkening sky, landing softly on the frost-covered ground.

The approach of Christmas, only nine days away, carried with it the promise of hope, as if all the wishes and dreams of a lifetime were within reach. And yet, not quite close enough to grasp and wouldn't be until Hayes assured himself his brother would get through whatever was coming.

CHAPTER SIX

The next day, it took three men six hours to axe through the top layer of hard earth and dig a hole sufficient for Pete Chase's coffin. By unspoken agreement, since no one suggested otherwise, he was buried outside the cemetery proper, though the reverend spoke over his grave as the coffin was lowered into the ground.

Judgment, he reminded them all, was not theirs to pass.

Like the Whitcombs, Cooper, Taylor, Elijah, and Hayes, Savannah had watched, listened, and waited until the reverend gave his final blessing. Once the others had left, Savannah stood at the edge of the town's cemetery, enveloped by a chilling breeze that whispered through the air.

Her eyes were drawn to the sight of stone markers and wooden crosses, their surfaces dusted with a delicate layer of frost. As she stepped closer to one, her fingertips brushed against the rough texture of the cold stone, the etched words indicating the woman who rested there had died in childbirth along with her infant son. The distant sound of bare branches rustling in the frigid breeze broke the solemn silence and dreariness.

However, Savannah couldn't help but imagine the transformation to come into this place of eternal rest as the seasons changed. In the vibrant embrace of spring, a picturesque view of majestic mountains would adorn the cemetery, serving as a backdrop to a meadow that would come alive with new growth. A carpet of lush, green grass and colorful wildflowers would paint a serene landscape, creating a peaceful sanctuary of solace and tranquility.

Her faith had never faltered, not once during four years of war, though faith seemed more elusive when her heart ached every time she caught a stray look from Hayes. She felt his anger as though it consumed her mind as the rapid beats of her heart mirrored his own whenever he looked toward the snowy mountains beyond the meadow, wondering if today the Devlin gang would set their sights on Whitcomb Springs.

One night and a new day had passed, and still efforts to find the outlaws had been unsuccessful, even with Elijah's help. Cooper picked up their tracks before another snow blew in and thwarted the search.

Hayes had moved into the hotel's only remaining room on the second floor, overlooking the town's main road and a clear sight of the clinic, though he spent only enough time in his room to freshen up before returning to Savannah's side or meeting with Cooper. As far as she could tell, he did not spend any time alone with his brother. Then again, she had not seen Elijah since the burial.

As the wind blew outside the clinic walls, Savannah spooned a tablespoon of honey mixed with lemon and cinnamon into six-year-old Davey Cox's mouth and handed him a clean handkerchief for his runny nose as she addressed his mother. "Twice a day, and a bowl of water hot enough to create steam by his bed at night."

"That is all?"

"It is." Savannah ruffled Davey's unruly hair when he made a face over his distaste of the concoction. "I will prepare you a bottle, enough for three days. Dried lemon peel and cinnamon sticks are soaked in honey for weeks. It is a better option for children and mild cases of cough or congestion."

Mrs. Cox, though skeptical, accepted the small bottle.

"It is Dr. Walker's preferred treatment. Why don't you bring Davey by the day after tomorrow for a follow-up with the doctor, and if you have any questions, please come in at any time."

Davey gave Savannah a toothy grin. "It's not so bad now."

Savannah helped him off the examination table. "Next time, mind your ma when she tells you to bundle up in the cold."

Smiling now, Mrs. Cox thanked Savannah, wrapped her son up in his coat, scarf, and mittens, and hurried him from the clinic and down the road to their house.

"You're good with children."

Savannah turned and assessed Hayes. His eyes lacked the brightness benefited by a full night's sleep, and three days without shaving left him with a ruggedness that should have made him appear unkept. Instead, the look flattered him, though Savannah kept the observation to herself. "I like most children."

He chuckled. "'Most' sounds about right. Have you ever wanted any of your own?"

A warmth radiated in her chest, rising up her neck to flush her cheeks. Yes, she had thought of having children once, long ago, with Hayes. When she imagined a future with him, building a home and life, the children they'd create. The dream faded with their parting, and never in the years since did she imagine such a life with anyone else.

Now . . . Savannah willed her tongue's cooperation so as to avoid tripping over her words. "I have always been fond of miracles."

And bless him, he understood. Hayes held out his hand. Savannah crossed the room to him and slid into his embrace. "When this is over—"

The clinic door pushed in, hitting the wall before Elijah kicked it closed behind him. "They want the money." He peered from Savannah to his brother. "Sorry. I can come back later."

"Too late." Hayes eased his hold on Savannah without releasing her. "The Devlins want the money? We already know, Elijah."

Elijah breathed into his hands and rubbed them together. "No, they want Whitcomb. Well, Whitcomb and his money."

"Daniel Whitcomb?" Savannah asked.

"Yes." Elijah passed them both and stopped in front of the stove, his hands extended. "Savannah, you were right. I lost my sense." He stomped his feet and inched closer to the heat.

"Why?" This time Hayes posed the question. At Elijah's blank look, Hayes added, "Not why you lost your sense. Daniel Whitcomb. Why him?"

"Days like this, I really miss Charleston." Elijah slipped his hands beneath his arms. "Wayne Devlin's brother died in Whitcomb's mine. Summer."

"Maurice?"

"No, Jake, the youngest."

"You went back to the Devlins." Hayes turned his brother to face him. "If you knew where to find them, why the hell didn't you tell us?"

"I swear, I didn't know they'd be there. When the snow started again and we had to return to town, I remembered Percy Glass mentioned one of their hideouts nearby. I hadn't been there before, and if I told Cooper and no one was there, well, it made sense to check it out first."

Hayes stared at his brother, his jaw clenched tight.

"I know, foolish. I wanted to make things right, to prove myself to you, to prove to this town that I'm trying to help."

The silence stretched between them, heavy with unspoken words. Hayes ran a hand through his hair, conflicting emotions warring within him. Part of him wanted to embrace his brother, to forgive and forget. But disappointment held him back. "From this second forward, you cannot keep anything from Cooper or us, Elijah."

"Understood, and I promise."

Hayes took his coat and hat off pegs by the door, and said to Savannah, "When is Taylor due back?"

"He was called away to another birthing, and there is no estimating when he will return." Savannah reached out to grasp Hayes's hand before he slipped into a glove. "Go ahead. Daniel needs to be warned. If this was all part of their plan—"

"Beg pardon, Savannah, but don't mistake them entirely. They want revenge for their brother, and they're also greedy enough to take the money if they can get to it. I'd say their thirst for retribution has more to do with making the Whitcombs pay—in any way possible."

❄

Hayes stepped out of the hotel the following morning. He'd slept for six hours, which was five hours more than the past three nights. Sunlight peeked through white clouds and glistened off the snow, forcing him to adjust his eyes and stay in the shadow of the hotel's covered front porch while he assessed the goings-on.

Though still cold, townspeople crossed the road, moving from one building to another. An old sleigh carrying a pile of small pine trees glided across the snow toward the church, the team of four horses holding their heads high. A woman carried a basket of ribbons and the man next to her pushed a handcart of greenery.

The scent of fresh bread wafted from an open door somewhere, reminding Hayes he hadn't eaten much since his brother's arrival. He had watched Savannah eat during their quiet meal last evening in the café but touched little of it himself.

His smile wavered when he caught sight of Cooper McCord crossing the road from the telegraph office. He stepped off the hotel's porch and waved to Cooper, who changed direction and met Hayes partway.

Cooper tucked his thumbs in his pockets and rocked back on his heels. "We're headed out again soon. This weather should hold a day or two at least."

Hayes peered up at the clear, blue sky. "How can you tell?"

"Does the air feel different than yesterday?"

"It's drier."

Cooper nodded. "And warmer, though that's harder to gauge."

Hayes's gaze drifted to the clinic, wondering if Savannah was still inside or if she'd finally gone home to rest.

Cooper interrupted Hayes's thoughts. "I spoke with Daniel before sending a wire to the territory marshal. Daniel and his wife were in Boston this past summer when Jake Devlin died, and only learned of it after the young man's parents picked Jake's body up. He went by Jake Fisher, so no connection was made. Turns out Devlin is their mother's surname."

Hayes shifted his attention back to Cooper. "Sounds like the younger brother was looking to distance himself."

"That's the size of it." Cooper scratched his unshaven chin with a gloved hand. "How's the injury?"

"I already have a doctor." Hayes rolled his shoulders, felt no uncomfortable tug. "It will hold. Have you seen Elijah? He didn't come to the hotel last night."

"He bunked at the jail."

"Huh." Hayes scanned the buildings and found the small jailhouse, which he doubted saw much regular use. "Voluntarily?"

"I had to make sure he wasn't going to ride off again, and I'll make no apologies for it."

"I suppose that's fair. Has he been sprung?"

"Short while ago. He's helping the others prepare the horses and supplies. There are only five of us riding out. Any more, and the Devlins will scatter, only to return another day. No lawman in the territory wants to be chasing them through the rest of winter." Cooper stepped aside when a young family walked nearby, dragging a small sleigh. He waited for them to pass before adding, "We need to bring the Devlins and their men in alive, or at least try."

Killing had not come easily to Hayes, at least in the beginning. The first time he knew a bullet from his rifle had hit its target, he sickened on the battlefield and considered deserting. The second time, he hadn't been sick, but the knot of fear that had formed in his stomach that first time clung to him like a shadow, enduring the relentless turmoil of the next three and a half years of war.

As he contemplated taking another life, the first time came flooding back, and with it, the internal struggle.

"My first captain—he died at Bull Run—used to tell his men, 'In the pursuit of justice, we forge the courage to demand what is right, not just for ourselves, but for the souls of those who can no longer exact justice for themselves.'" Hayes tugged at his gloves, lifted his face briefly to the sunlight, and asked himself, 'What would Savannah want him to do?' "All right. Tell me the plan."

CHAPTER SEVEN

"What am I doing wrong?" Two days later, Savannah found herself in Evelyn Whitcomb's kitchen, wrist-deep in flour, sticky dough, and frustration. Her apron wore more flour than the cloth covering the long table in the kitchen.

Abigail peered around her shoulder, stifled a laugh, and shrugged. "It looks better than my first try at pie crust."

Evelyn *tsked* at her sister and moved to Savannah's side. She stifled her laugh better than Abigail had. "It is much better than Abigail's first try. Hers would have made an excellent doorstop had I not been keen on inviting ants into the house. Not to worry, we can salvage the crust."

Evelyn showed her how to add flour, a little at a time, until the sticky dough turned soft. "Now, it will flatten easily so long as you keep the roller lightly floured. Don't press down too hard, though, and lift as you roll right to the edge so the crust is even."

Savannah watched Evelyn complete three steady rolls

across what she hoped would be an edible pie crust before taking over. "This isn't working."

"You are doing a beautiful job."

"I am not referring to the dough." Savannah agreed, though, that it was coming along nicely. "The distraction is not as distracting as you hoped."

"With the first three pies already done for the hotel, and with your pecan pie, and my—" Abigail looked around the kitchen. "Where are the canned apples?"

"In the first pie you made," Evelyn said. "That one is going to be spiced peach. The filling is on the stove."

"Well, never mind." Abigail smoothed a palm over her rolled crust before folding it in quarters and setting the corner in the center of a prepared dish. "Distracted or not, Savannah, it is passing the time, and with the hotel's regular cook on bed rest with that awful head cold, the guests will appreciate all these pies. Sally Lowell was kind to step in to help. She makes a wonderful stew and bakes a ham to perfection, but by her own admission has yet to make a dessert her husband can keep down." Abigail wiped the excess flour from her hands and glanced at Savannah's efforts. "Your crust is looking splendid."

Savannah finished rolling, and pleased enough with the results, shrugged. "I have not made a pie since I was fifteen and my mother permitted our cook to show me the basics of working in a kitchen. My skills have deteriorated since that long-ago lesson."

"You have other important skills." Evelyn talked Savannah through spooning the prepared filling into the crust and fluting the crust edges. "There, the hard part is over."

No, Savannah thought, the hard part wouldn't be over until Hayes and the other men returned. Her only comfort was knowing the sun graced them with its presence for another day. However, according to Jeb, who looks after the Whitcomb's horses and broke his leg three years prior, they were in for another storm within two, maybe three, days.

Hayes had surprised her at her cabin before he left, while she still wore her white flannel nightgown and a single braid over her shoulder. He pulled her against him, kissed her fiercely, and left with a whispered promise, "I will return to you." She recalled watching him mount the horse Cooper loaned him. If his wound still pained him, he hid it well.

When a full day and night passed without a word from Hayes, Savannah felt as though the space around her became smaller and smaller. "Please tell me they are alive."

Evelyn sat at the table next to Savannah while Abigail refreshed the tea in their cups. Evelyn said, "They know what they are doing, and if it was too dangerous, Cooper would have stopped them and returned home. No one knows the mountains better, and there is no one Daniel and I trust more with any of our lives than Abigail's husband."

Savannah circled her fingers around the teacup, savoring the warmth. "How far away is the mine? I have never been there."

"Too far to walk, and you may not take the sleigh or a horse." Evelyn clasped her hand. "We have all been in your situation, wondering if those we love will return safely home, considering how we might help, what else we could do instead of sitting and waiting."

"And still we wait." Abigail checked on the pecan pie's progress in the oven before joining them at the table. "When I first met Cooper, I was up a tree to avoid a bear." She held up a hand. "And yes, I realize bears can climb trees, but it was not one of the many things going through my mind. To Cooper, the bear was a mere nuisance, nothing to worry about. It is the same look he gave me before he left yesterday." All three women looked at the ceiling when a gleeful shout of "Ma!" sounded through the house.

"And that will be the children up." Abigail swiped a stray hair from her face. "Daniel Jr. will awaken Lizzie if he doesn't—and there she goes. Excuse me. Evelyn, I'll get Daniel Jr. cleaned up."

Savannah smiled at Evelyn when Abigail left the room. "You are both sweet and not at all reassuring. I trust Cooper, and still . . ." She pressed a fist over her heart. "I cannot stop the tightness and flutters from overwhelming me." The room felt suffocating, the air heavy with spice and warmth from the stove. The sight of her friends' concerned faces only intensified the knot in her stomach. "I should like a walk."

When she rose, Evelyn also stood and held Savannah's arm. "Promise you will not go far."

Savannah considered, then said, "I promise not to venture farther than I should." Which wasn't the response Evelyn hoped to hear. Still, she did not stop her from leaving when Savannah rolled down her sleeves, donned her outer clothing, and stepped onto Evelyn's front porch.

She loved the view from this spot and wondered how her friend accomplished anything when she could sit or stand in this place and savor the peacefulness. The mountains somehow appeared taller today, their peaks heavily coated in snow covering all traces of rock and trees.

Ignoring the pounding in her chest and at the edge of her temples, Savannah walked down the four steps to the road and started toward the clinic. She could lose herself in work more easily than in baking pies. For so long now, she used her hands to heal, and only when necessity demanded it did she use them to prepare food.

Since her arrival in Whitcomb Springs, she had become one of the café's most reliable patrons. When necessary, she could scramble eggs, toast bread, or fry potatoes, though often, all three burned. No, she shouldn't be baking pies, at least not while Hayes was somewhere out in the cold, unable to enjoy them.

She shook her head at her own foolish thoughts and kicked the snow off her boots before stepping up to the clinic door. The blast halted her movement. As she gripped the cold, metal handle of the door with one hand, she could feel the chill seep through her glove, making her fingers tingle. She waited. Had it been her imagination? A planned explosion at the mine? Another blast, this one unmistakably the echo of gunfire, the sound reverberating through the air. Her legs wobbled like a frail sapling in a fierce storm, even though the ground itself did not shake. She turned at the sound of shouts and frantic movement behind her.

The clinic door opened, Savannah nearly tumbling inward with it. Taylor caught her against him and righted her again. He stepped outside, without a coat, and watched the bustling activity. He placed his hands on her shoulders and turned her. There, above the trees flocked with snow, a thin stream of smoke rose into the air.

"Is that the mine?"

Taylor nodded. "I'll get my bag. I need you to stay here." When he turned a minute later, this time wearing a coat, Abigail had nearly reached them. She wore only a heavy wool shawl, her cheeks reddened from the cold.

Nearly out of breath from running, Abigail said, "Jeb

and a group of men are headed to the mine. Evelyn wanted me to make sure you don't try to follow them."

Taylor closed the clinic door behind him. "Make sure she doesn't." To Savannah he said, "You can help Hayes best by staying safe."

"Hayes." His name left her lips on a soft breath as she watched the smoke thicken.

He closed his eyes and whispered, "Savannah." Her name left a sweet taste on his lips, his mouth remembering their parting kiss and his promise. Hayes leaned with his back against the base of a larch, its golden needles long since dropped and buried beneath the snow.

"Do you see them?"

Cooper leaned against the tree next to Hayes and nodded. "Two of them, on the north side of the mine shaft entrance, and these trees aren't enough protection." Cooper shifted to stand sideways against the tree. He aimed between the two trunks and fired a shot. A scream rent the air. "About time."

Hayes shifted, aimed, and fired, shooting only the hat off his quarry. Whoever he almost hit shouted a profanity. "Smart men would have ridden off as soon as two of their own were captured."

"Yes, they would have. Daniel should almost be back to town by now with Percy and Roscoe. The others went with him, so no one is getting to him."

Cooper nodded. "We bring them in tied up or dead. And it has to end soon because I have no intention of spending another night away from my wife."

Hayes said nothing at first, his breath visible in the crisp, winter air. The silence was deafening, like a heavy blanket pressing down on him. "If they wanted revenge for the brother's death, why are the Devlins still here? They should be following Daniel."

Cooper raised a finger to his mouth in a signal of silence. He closed his eyes and listened. When he opened his eyes, he looked in the direction opposite of the shooting. "They aren't alone."

Hayes swore. "Elijah said there were only four of them."

"Not any longer, and I'd wager the Devlin brothers aren't the ones we've been shooting at. They're a decoy."

They ran for their horses, mounted, and rode the animals as quickly as the snow allowed until they passed through the tree line and reached the wide trail leading from the mine to town. Shots fired from behind, skimming the air and hitting nothing as Hayes and Cooper gave the animals their heads.

CHAPTER EIGHT

Savannah no longer sensed she was alone. Her head snapped up, and she stepped back at the unexpected sight of a face in the clinic window. Evelyn Whitcomb mouthed a quick, "Sorry," before walking to the door and coming inside. "I am so sorry to have startled you."

She waved away Evelyn's concern even as she held a palm to her chest. "I was preoccupied with my own thoughts." Savannah dropped the old cloth she'd been using to dust into the dirty linens bucket for the laundry. "You come with your hands full."

Evelyn held up a basket as she carried it to the kitchen area and set it on a table. "Muffins. You so rarely leave the clinic these days, except for dinner. I asked Maggie over at the tavern to have some of their bean stew and corn bread sent over. No one in town makes it better."

"Thank you, Evelyn. This is thoughtful of you, as you always are." Savannah suspected she looked a mess and took a moment to smooth her hair and apron. "I suppose . . ." She glanced at the clock and realized four hours and twenty-two minutes had passed since she left Evelyn's house . . . since the explosion. "It has been longer than I realized." Savannah could not keep the hopefulness out of her eyes when she asked, "Has there been any word?"

"That is the other reason I am here." Evelyn partially uncovered the muffins, found a plate within easy reach on a shelf with cups and miscellaneous dishes and cutlery. "I will consider it a kindness if you sit and eat this. It is one of the café's best apple cinnamon muffins. There are also berry if you prefer, but I was told the apple are your favorite." Evelyn set a fork next to the muffin.

Savannah acquiesced when her stomach protested its morning fasting. "What news have you heard?"

"Daniel has returned. They've captured two of the men."

Savannah's fork clattered on the dish and landed on the table. "Hayes?"

"He is still with Cooper. Elijah returned with Daniel and the other two who had ridden with them. As Daniel explained it, Cooper and Hayes rode north and when they found the Devlin gang, they lured them using themselves—"

"Bait for a trap." She stood, knocking the chair backward. "I swear if women ruled the world—"

"Yes, we have all thought what you are thinking." Evelyn moved behind Savannah to right the chair. "The explosion was a diversion, and it worked, except the Devlin brothers are still out there."

"Why did Daniel return?"

"He promised Cooper, though he told me he'll be heading back out with Elijah as soon as the two they caught

—Percy and Roscoe he called them—are securely behind bars. Daniel is also wiring the marshal again."

A chill swept through the room, making Savannah shiver despite the warmth from the stove. She wrapped her arms around herself, an inexplicable sense of dread settling in her stomach. A floorboard creaked somewhere in the clinic, and both women froze. Savannah's heart pounded in her chest as she strained to listen. The silence that followed was deafening, broken only by wind pushing against the windows.

Evelyn's eyes widened, and she pressed a finger to her lips. Savannah nodded, her breath caught in her throat. Another creak echoed through the clinic, closer this time. The women exchanged glances.

Savannah inched toward the desk, her hand trembling as she reached for the drawer where she knew Taylor kept a small pistol. Just as her fingers grasped the handle, a shadow fell across the doorway.

The floorboards groaned under heavy footsteps. A deep, gravelly voice cut through the silence. "You don't want to do that, ma'am."

Savannah turned, her hand still on the drawer, to face the man. Snow dusted his black felt hat and the shoulders of his dark-brown coat. His boots left damp prints on the floorboards. She almost asked how he got in, but she already knew, and cursed herself for a fool for leaving the back door unlocked after she returned from her cabin.

"There is nothing here you could want. No money, and the doctor doesn't even keep much morphine on hand. You are welcome to whatever is in the cupboards."

He pointed the barrel of his pistol at Savannah, then at Evelyn. "Whose cabin is out back?"

He stepped toward them.

"It is mine." Savannah sidled closer to Evelyn, putting herself between her friend and the gun.

"We're going for a walk." He motioned with his free hand for them to move.

Evelyn wouldn't stay behind her. They kept as much distance between them and the man as possible as they moved toward the hallway. "You are one of the Devlins, are you not? Where is your brother?"

Savannah nudged Evelyn to keep quiet. Evelyn, however, ignored her. "What do you hope to gain from this? If it is money, we will pay it."

The man's eyes narrowed. "I'll ask the questions. Now, move."

The floorboards creaked beneath their feet, and as they neared the back door, the man roughly shoved them forward. "Open it," he growled, gesturing toward the door with his pistol.

With shaking hands, Savannah reached for the handle. As the door swung open, the wind blew against them, and without a cloak or even a shawl, the frigid cold whipped her hair and seeped through her clothes.

Savannah tripped out the back door, and though Evelyn grabbed hold of her arm, she slipped and fell face forward, her arms out to brace the fall. "Savannah!" Evelyn took a hurried step forward, only to be pulled back by her coat, her back slamming into the man's chest.

Savannah righted herself, first coming up on all fours, then fighting the drag of her wet skirts as she pushed against her cold, chafed hands to stand. Enough of the pins holding her hair in its customary loose knot had fallen out so that now most of her dark locks fell down her back and over one shoulder in disarray. "Is this what you think a real man does? Frighten and threaten women? Are you so weak that you must hold a gun on us?"

"Savannah." Evelyn spoke her name with a sharp edge.

The man yanked Evelyn closer to him. "You looking to get both of you killed?"

She avoided eye contact with Evelyn, her hard gaze focused on the man, even as her mind filled with a silent prayer for strength. "I'd rather die on my feet than cower to you."

A tense silence fell over the narrow clearing between the clinic and Savannah's cabin, broken only by the rustle of branches and the distant call of a hawk. The man's eyes remained on Savannah, clearly unsure how to handle her unexpected bravado.

Approaching hoofbeats echoed off the structures and through the trees, giving Savannah a single swift chance when his head snapped around, distracted.

Savannah scooped up a handful of snow and rock and flung it directly into the man's face. He cursed, wiped at his eyes and face, and lost his grip on Evelyn just long enough for her to rush outside. He fired half-blind, missing her, but he was still faster—and stronger.

The man landed against Savannah's back as the women ran. Shouts, no doubt brought on by the sound of gunfire, were drowned out by the ringing in her ears when she landed on the ground, with the man's heavy body covering her back and half her legs.

"Savannah!"

"Go, Evelyn! Now!"

"You stupid—"

Savannah's elbow connected with his side. The first time he cursed and returned the hit. The second time, she hit him hard enough to roll away. His cry of pain was what finally broke through the ringing as her eyes adjusted. She wiped her face the best she could with a damp sleeve and hands still too cold to nimbly move her fingers.

"Savannah?"

A voice she recognized, the soft and husky timbre from which she drew comfort, and the arms of the man she loved lifted her up and out of the snow. Hayes held her against him, his face against hers, as he carried her not to the clinic but to her cabin. He set her down only long enough to remove the key from the chain around her neck and unlock the door.

Hayes carried her inside and kicked the door closed. Savannah vaguely heard Evelyn shouting her name mingled with commotion beyond the walls of her cabin. She didn't care about any of it.

Savannah hesitated to release her fierce grip on Hayes's shirt when he laid her on the settee and covered her with a dark-green, knit throw she kept across the back. He said nothing to her as he started a fire in the hearth. Once the flame grew to his satisfaction, he left her for the kitchen. She heard the sound of the water pump followed by the heavy clank of the kettle being set on the cookstove.

When he returned, Hayes stood at the threshold, watching her. The firelight caught the first glint of moisture in his eyes, and she immediately held out her hand to him, moving her legs off the settee to make room for him. Instead of sitting, he kneeled and gathered her in his embrace.

A dozen platitudes of reassurance slipped into her thoughts only to be rejected, for nothing, save the steady beat of her heart, would convince him she was safe. He tightened his grip, and she released a low moan of pain. Hayes pulled back.

"You're hurt. Where?" Hayes clenched his jaw, his handsome face marred by fresh scratches.

With each shallow breath, she felt the sting of her bruised ribs, and still managed a smile for his benefit. Savannah cupped his face and skimmed her thumb over a scratch. "How did you come by these?"

"Bullets hit the tree I was hiding behind. Those are from the bark," he answered, while he checked her arms, back, and legs for injury. She allowed him the freedom to do so.

"Hayes, I am fine." Savannah leaned forward and pressed her lips to his. "I promise. You arrived before he could hurt either of us." Now that she had some modicum of control over her wits, Savannah asked, "How did you know?"

Without releasing her, Hayes finally sat next to her and readjusted the throw to cover her again. "I feel like the last —I don't even know how long it's been—happened to someone else. Daniel and the others returned with two of the Devlins' men, and Cooper and I had, we thought, the Devlins cornered. Cooper realized otherwise at the same time I felt something was wrong. We left whoever was out there. We were riding into the center of town, to warn Daniel, when we heard the shot behind the clinic."

Hayes kissed her hard and lifted her onto his lap. "When I saw him fall on you, I thought it was the bullet that took you down." He buried his face against her neck. "I swore when I found you again that I'd never let anything happen to you, and still you almost—"

Savannah pressed a finger firmly to his mouth. "We have both seen and lived through too much to know you cannot protect me from every what-if and might-be in the world. We will, of course, try every day to do so." She let her body sink against his. "I want to return here, to this place and relive this moment with you." Savannah eased away slightly. "First, I need to ensure myself Evelyn is unharmed, and is there not still another Devlin brother missing?"

Hayes took her hand and kissed the palm, a feathery brush of his lips followed by a smile. "I am in awe of you. All right, we'll finish what needs to be done, if you promise to let Dr. Walker check your ribs. It is your ribs, isn't it?"

Savannah nodded. "Agreed."

CHAPTER NINE

"You'll be fine." Taylor washed his hands at the basin and dried them off while Savannah buttoned her bodice over her chemise. "I want you to stay away from the clinic for at least two days. Rest. Walking is fine, but don't lift anything."

She smiled behind his back when she slid off the examination table. His bedside manner usually held more hint of sugar than starch, though Savannah didn't mind. She recalled the color seeping from his face when Hayes carried her into the clinic and told Taylor to help her while he found Daniel and Cooper.

An hour later and Taylor still hadn't let go of all his anger. Savannah understood that Taylor's concern and guilt stemmed from the dangerous situation she'd been in, and he hadn't been there to protect her.

"I will tell you what I have said before, and what Hayes is reluctantly realizing: You cannot keep me wrapped up, safe from all the world's dangers."

"It won't stop me from trying." Taylor tossed the towel

in a basket with other rags to be picked up by the laundress who twice weekly washed the clinic's linens.

"I know." She crossed to him, stood on the toes of her boots, and kissed his cheek. "Hayes said much the same." Savannah turned, arms raised. "See, I am better already."

"Humph."

She smiled again. "Do you know where Hayes might have gone? If I am not allowed to work, I will enjoy the sunshine. You see," she pointed to the window, "the sun is bright when not an hour ago dark clouds threatened another storm. It is the small joys, Taylor, which make every moment worth hoping for another beautiful day."

He finally smiled, as she hoped he would. "You can't go to Hayes right now." Taylor gathered fresh cloths and instruments he'd washed and placed them in his medical bag.

"Are you off to another house call?"

Taylor nodded, his back straight, his muscles moving out of memory, and his eyes edged with exhaustion. "Someone slipped a note under the door while I was out, before Hayes brought you in here. Molly Greenhow started birthing pains this morning."

"The widow who lives on the farm south of town?" Savannah had met her twice, both times briefly. She remembered Molly's husband died from exposure two months ago while hunting, and the woman had no other family.

"She does." Taylor shrugged on his coat, wrapping a thick wool scarf twice around his neck. "Last week, Abigail tried to convince her to move into town. The Whitcombs converted one of the rooms above the general store for her, but she wants the baby born in the house her husband built."

Savannah hadn't known that. Of course, since Haye's arrival, her thoughts rarely veered from him. "I want to go with you." When Taylor shook his head, she pressed. "I will not lift, bend, or overly exert myself. Please, Taylor, I need to be of use to someone right now."

With one hand on his medical bag and the other on the door handle, Taylor looked at her. "That's the most you've said my given name at one time." His mouth curved. "It's progress. Despite the sun, it's still freezing out there. Wear one of the extra flannel shirts in the hall bureau under your cloak. We'll borrow the sleigh from the livery."

One minute later, Savannah was dressed to his satisfaction. She gave him a jaunty salute when she presented herself, bringing forth a chuckle. When she stepped outside and Taylor closed and locked the door behind her, Savannah attempted to keep a jovial mood on the short walk between the clinic and livery. However, her gaze darted every which way, never catching a glimpse of the person she most wanted to see.

"Where are they? Do you know?"

"Yes, I know." He didn't stop, only took hold of her arm and moved her out of the way of a horse and rider. "And no, I won't tell you. Not yet. Will you trust me?"

She studied him for several heartbeats before nodding. "Always."

They stomped snow off their shoes when they reached the livery. The sleigh and team of two was readied, and within fifteen minutes, Taylor drove the team onto the flattened snow for the quarter-mile ride to the Greenhow farm.

Hayes stood to one side of Maurice Devlin, Cooper on the other, and Daniel in front of the man sitting on the narrow cot in the jail cell. The town only boasted one, and from what Cooper explained, it was often empty—until now. Percy and Roscoe kept to one end, each shackled to the bars while they spoke with Maurice.

"Where's Wayne?"

Maurice laughed, a hard, humorless sound. "Why'd you think I'd tell you anything?"

"Because," Cooper said, "you're smart enough to know you won't be getting out of this. You will be picked up by the marshals, and you will end up in the prison."

"Is that the one in Utah?" Daniel asked Cooper.

"Could be, but it's too easy to escape from there. Now, seeing as how most of the mine owners the Devlins and their crew have stolen from are Easterners with influence, I expect they'll be shipped east, to someplace more secure. There are plenty to choose from out there." Cooper shrugged. "Thankfully, it's not our mess. We could be persuaded to tell the marshal you cooperated, but . . ." Cooper leaned against the bars.

"You don't have the authority."

Daniel nodded. "True. I hear Helena's Vigilantes have joined the hunt for you. Now that we've sent word you're in custody, the marshal might make it before they do. They are more likely to hang you than you turn you over to the law."

Maurice fought against the ropes around his legs and holding his arms, unmoving, against his torso. "You can't do that!"

"Where's your brother?" Hayes asked. He would never condone vigilante justice, and didn't think either Cooper or Daniel would, either, yet it was an effective threat. Maurice avoided looking at Percy and Boscoe at the other end of the cell. Those men had already talked before Maurice joined them.

"It don't matter where." Maurice spit on the jail floor. "He'll be coming for me, and then he'll kill you, Daniel Whitcomb."

Daniel motioned Hayes out of the cell. Cooper pushed off the bars, unsheathed a long blade from a leather scabbard at his back, and walked toward Maurice as Daniel joined Hayes. "You and your brother won't have your revenge. Not today, not here. You've underestimated us."

"Another minute with those women and I would've—"

Cooper's single punch silenced Maurice, who slumped over and rolled off the cot. Cooper sliced through the ropes while Daniel walked around the outside of the cell and unlocked Percy and Boscoe. As the men were freed, Cooper was locking the cell door.

The three men went to the front room, closed the door. Hayes said, "I expect you want to keep this between us."

Daniel nodded. "My fight doesn't need to become the town's. Elijah and Jeb are keeping watch at my house. Evelyn and Abigail will be safe there with the children. I'm riding out to find Wayne Devlin."

Cooper and Hayes barely glanced at each other before each saying their own version of, "Let's go."

CHAPTER TEN

Savannah mopped Molly Greenhow's brow with a damp cloth she kept dipping in cool water. Still, sweat beaded on Molly's temple, and when the time came for her to scream and push, she merely rolled her head side to side and moaned.

"Taylor?"

"The baby hasn't turned."

Two women from town waited in the kitchen while their husbands waited outside in the barn, entering the house only to replenish the coffee in their cups and warm their hands by the fire. Savannah couldn't blame them. The noises coming from Molly sounded like a dying animal, and since both men had children of their own, they'd likely been through this before.

Evelyn confessed that if her son's birthing had lasted any longer, Daniel might have fainted. Savannah tried to conjure the humor from Evelyn's retelling, but she only saw Molly, a widow about to bring a child into the world to raise alone.

Taylor pressed a palm on Molly's belly as he tried to turn the baby inside. "Molly, can you hear me?"

Molly moaned in response.

Savannah leaned close to Molly's ear and said, "Molly, can you open your eyes?"

Another moan.

"Taylor, can you get the baby out?"

He wiped his hands and glanced at his medical bag. "If I go in through her stomach, the baby might have a chance."

It's what he didn't say that troubled Savannah. "And Molly." The desolation reflecting in his eyes was answer enough. "Can you save them both?"

Molly reached out and grabbed Savannah's arm, her grip surprisingly firm and her eyes remarkably lucid now. "Save the baby."

Savannah covered Molly's hand. "We need to save you both, Molly. Your child will need you."

"Save the baby. Please."

Molly's head listed to the side. "She's fainted."

Taylor leaned forward, took hold of one of Molly's hands, and pressed two fingers to her wrist. "There's no pulse."

Savannah shook Molly gently. "Molly, wake up, please. Molly! Can't anything be done?"

Taylor raised Molly's nightgown to above her belly, then poured alcohol on his hands and a scalpel. "Yes. We can save her baby."

Savannah turned her head away before Taylor made the cut. Instead, she watched Molly, unmoving, the color draining from her face with each passing second.

"I need your hands, Savannah."

She turned back and her breath caught.

"Now!"

Savannah hurried to the doctor's side, picked up the blanket set out for just this moment, and held steady when Taylor lowered the infant onto the soft cloth. "He's not breathing."

Taylor said nothing as he clamped the cord, massaged the baby's neck, and tilted Savannah's arms toward him so the baby rested at an angle. In less time than it took for Savannah to release her pent-up breath, the infant boy announced his existence with a quiet cry, which quickly turned into a wail.

Only when a tear dropped onto her hand did Savannah realize she was crying. Every pain, every heartache, every horror in the world ceased to exist in this precious moment. She brought herself around long enough to see Taylor at Molly's side, checking for any sign of life. When his eyes met hers, he slowly shook his head, lowered Molly's gown, and raised the bed quilt to cover her completely.

He circled the bed and returned to the baby. Savannah held the child patiently while Taylor cut the cord and cleaned the newborn. "Do they have a cow or goat here?"

"One of the women who came is still nursing her infant. She said she'd be willing to help. Abigail organized women to rotate coming out here after Molly refused to come into town." Taylor took the baby from Savannah's arms and carried him from the room. Seconds later, footsteps sounded in the hall and another door opened and closed.

When he returned, she asked, "Was Molly in danger before the birthing?"

Taylor washed his hands and gathered everything he had brought with him. "Molly had been weak the past month, losing weight, showing no interest in getting out of bed. I worried about her ability to care for the baby after the birth."

"And now? What will happen with the baby?"

"Molly's husband once told me, when I treated him for burns after his forge blew up, that he and Molly were alone, and they looked forward to having a big family." Taylor secured the straps on his medical bag. "All we can do now is give Molly a proper burial and find the child a loving home."

Savannah stopped Taylor from leaving with a gentle touch to his arm. "How long do you expect to keep going as you have been?"

"For as long as it takes."

Hayes stared down into the gully, watching the water freely flow over and around rocks as the frigid stream occasionally carried away snow from off the sloped banks. "It looks like your bullet hit true, Cooper. Are you sure this is Wayne Devlin?"

Cooper nodded. "Matches his description, and I see the resemblance to his brother." He removed his hat long enough to rub a hand over his forehead. "I didn't want it to end this way."

Hayes estimated the daylight remaining and contemplated pulling the body from the gully. "I only see one set of tracks from a horse. He and whoever was with him likely separated at the mine."

"We'll find him." Marshal Pinney sat atop his horse on the opposite side of the gully, his hat low, his face red and chapped from the cold. Three men from his posse sat on horses on either side of him. "Foster," he said to the man on his right. "Ride back and find the others, have them come back here and pull out Wayne. We'll ride onto Whitcomb Springs to take the others into custody."

"You'll be welcome to them, Marshal." Daniel turned his horse first. Cooper and Hayes followed, leaving the marshal's men to deal with Wayne Devlin and to everyone's relief, Maurice, Percy, and Roscoe.

"One week until Christmas." Hayes smiled when he sighted the small mountain town he'd come to think of as home in such a short time. The tension pulling between his shoulders eased, the tightness behind his neck loosened, and when he took a deep breath, it was relief that now, finally, he could do what he intended since the moment he set out to find Savannah. "I can use your help with something, gentlemen, if you'd oblige me."

"Name it," Cooper said, as their horses followed their natural inclinations to find warmth and food.

"I may also need Evelyn and Abigail's help, and Elijah will want to help."

"Out with it." Daniel stopped at the corner where he and Cooper planned to part with Hayes.

"I'll call on you tomorrow."

CHAPTER ELEVEN

Savannah's delicate finger brushed over the downy fuzz atop baby Alexander's head before she carefully placed him in the cradle next to the settee. "We haven't discussed it," she whispered.

Hayes sat next to her, silent in his watching, his love for this woman having grown so much, yet knowing his heart still had room for even more of her and whoever came into their lives. "You told me what happened to Molly, and Abigail confirmed neither she nor her husband had any family, which is why they came west." The fire crackled and fragrant spices wafted from the kitchen where a pie baked in the oven. "Alexander. Was he someone you knew?"

Savannah leaned into Hayes and his arm draped over her shoulders. "He was the first soldier I helped save. Only nineteen. He came to the hospital with a hole in his side and leg already black from infection. Alexander lost the leg, but never once did he lose hope. Never before or since did I see a soldier with so much courage."

"Did he survive?"

"Yes. I wrote to him after the war and he replied with news of his engagement to the prettiest, sweetest girl ever to be born in Virginia. Alexander was also his father's name. Molly's husband. It seemed fate guided the choosing." Savannah wiped a tear from her cheek.

"It's a good, strong name, Savannah." Hayes brushed aside her hair and kissed her brow. "Have you already spoken with Daniel and Evelyn? I suppose they're as close to town officials as Whitcomb Springs has."

"I did. And they sent a wire to Atlanta, where the Greenhows lived before coming here. I selfishly wish they hadn't, but if baby Alexander has a real family out there, and they want him, then they deserve to know."

"He has family here, no matter what happens."

Savannah straightened. "You mean it."

"One child or a dozen." Hayes held her face still between his large hands and kissed her soundly. "We'll make room for them in our home and our hearts."

"Hope is love's compass, reminding us that tomorrow's dawn can cradle the promise of a brighter beginning." Savannah smoothed her sensitive fingertips over his cheek. "The matron at the last hospital where I worked said those words to me. A gift, she said, from her mother, and hers before. A stout Irishwoman who spoke a prayer over every soldier who entered the hospital doors. She found me crying in a supply closet after an especially brutal week in what turned out to be the last four weeks before the war's end. I etched those words in memory and have recalled them every time despair tried to overtake my soul."

Hayes wiped a tear from the soft skin below her eye, then smoothed his strong hands over her arms and settled at her waist. "Has it worked?"

Savannah leaned forward to kiss his forehead, the tip of

his nose, and finally pressed her lips to his as his arms wrapped around her waist and drew her close. She whispered against his mouth, "You are my compass now, Hayes."

"And you are my every dawn." His thumbs gently brushed away the traces of tears that had welled in her eyes, tears born of joy to match the love staring back at him.

A quick rap at the door separated them. Hayes stood from the settee, lifted her against him, and gave her one more heady kiss before holding her at arm's length.

When she opened her eyes and looked through the temporary daze into which he'd put her, she saw his grin. "The door. That will be Sarah to feed Alexander."

Hayes chuckled. "She'll be staying longer than a feeding. We have a wedding to get to, Miss Savannah Quinn." He led her to the front door and ushered Sarah inside. "We'll be off, Sarah."

"Of course. No need to rush back. My youngest fell off to sleep, so I've plenty of time."

Hayes winked at her as he helped Savannah on with her cloak and wrapped a wool scarf twice around her neck. "You need gloves."

"It is Christmas Eve, Hayes." She took the gloves from him and tugged them on herself and glanced at the clock on her fireplace mantel. "What is going on?" she asked of Hayes, but looked to Sarah, who had already settled next to the baby and said nothing.

"Come along. We'll be late."

Savannah, still blushing from moments earlier, and still warmed by his words—his every dawn indeed—she fought the urge between hitting him and delaying him with another kiss. "I didn't realize the time. Evelyn, Abigail, and

I are meeting at the church to prepare for the Christmas Eve feast. It is my first Christmas here and I want to do whatever I can to help. And there is no pending wedding in Whitcomb Springs, or it would be all anyone could speak about."

Hayes merely smiled and donned his own outer clothes. "Maybe you haven't been talking to the right people."

"I know everyone now—Hayes!"

He urged her out the front door, closing the door behind him. The icy late afternoon air did not deter his smile or enthusiasm. "Everyone doesn't know everything."

"That makes no sense."

"Sure it does." Hayes kept her to the front and side of him so he could help her over and around obstacles that might slow their progress. He barely slowed when they reached the church door. He opened it, got them inside, and closed it before Savannah could ask what he was doing. And she would have if what greeted them had not quite simply stolen the words from her mind.

The soft glow of candlelight flickered against the stone walls of the church while shadows danced in time with a soft piano melody in the background. Fresh evergreen boughs draped over the altar, their fragrant scent mingling with that of burning wax, spice, and wood in the corner stove. Behind the altar, an impressive evergreen stood nearly ten feet tall, its branches decked with ribbons, strings of dried fruit, and pinecones.

Except for the soft song, the player hidden just now by more evergreens and ribbons, Savannah heard nothing beyond the music and Hayes's soft breathing behind her. "You knew?"

He leaned close and whispered against her ear, "You also did a fair job distracting of me. I worried we'd be late."

"Late for what? It appears everything is already done."

Hayes stepped in front of her, took each of her hands in his to remove the gloves, then kissed each one. "Not quite." He dropped to one knee, transferring both her hands to one of his so he could reach into his shirt pocket. He held out a ring but did not slip it on her finger. The simple band adorned with a small yet sparkling emerald glistened in the candlelight. "My grandfather gave my grandmother this ring on the day of their wedding, and she wore it fifty-five years. I had it with me the day you told me you were leaving for Vermont."

Savannah leaned toward him, unable to cover a soft gasp as she remembered the picnic he'd planned.

"I buried it beneath my house during the war and have carried it every day since. No other woman is meant to wear this ring, until, I hope, one day our daughter wears it."

Savannah smiled even as soft tears fell down her cheeks. "Fifty-five years is a long time."

Hayes grinned up at her. "Not nearly long enough, but it's a good start. Will you accept me, Savannah Quinn? My devotion, my surrender, and my love have always been for you."

"Yes." Savannah tugged on his hands until he stood, only an inch between them. "If you accept mine."

At Hayes's loud whoop, Evelyn and Daniel, Abigail and Cooper, Taylor, Elijah, and the reverend filed into the chapel. The wooden floorboards creaked as their friends gathered in a semicircle. Evelyn passed a bouquet of cut greens, winterberry branches, and red ribbon to Savannah, before giving her a kiss on the cheek and a big smile. Elijah took up the space next to his brother as Hayes held fast to his bride's hand when they faced the altar.

As the reverend began the ceremony to bind her and

Hayes together, Savannah breathed in the scent of pine from her bouquet. The flickering candlelight cast a warm glow through the small chapel, illuminating the joyous faces of their friends. Savannah's heart raced as she listened to the reverend's words, her eyes never leaving Hayes's.

"Hayes," the reverend's voice brought her back to the present, "do you take Savannah to be your wedded wife?"

"I do," Hayes replied, his voice thick with emotion. His eyes sparkled as he gazed at Savannah, a smile playing at the corners of his mouth.

"And Savannah," the reverend continued, "do you take Hayes to be your wedded husband?"

Savannah took a deep breath, her eyes locked with Hayes's. "I do," she said, her voice clear and strong.

The reverend smiled warmly. "Then, by the power granted to me, I now pronounce you husband and wife. You may kiss the bride."

Hayes gently cupped Savannah's face in his hands and leaned in, pressing his lips to hers in a tender kiss. The chapel erupted in enthusiastic cheers and applause.

As they broke apart, Savannah laughed, her cheeks flushed with happiness. Hayes grinned and swept her into his arms, spinning her around. As their friends gathered closer to offer hugs, handshakes, and well-wishes, a warmth spread through Savannah's chest. She looked up at Hayes.

"We're finally home."

EPILOGUE

One year later
Christmas Eve, 1868

The church smelled of spiced apples, cinnamon cookies, and freshly baked bread. The hand-carved wooden pews had been moved to the edges of the room with enough space in the center for tables now laden with pies, both sweet and savory, soups, cakes, tarts, and more. Half already consumed and the rest of the repast enjoyed as laughter mingled with conversation and caroling.

Children played in one corner when they weren't sneaking extra desserts while their mothers were occupied. Hayes wrapped his arms around Savannah, protectively covering the gentle curve of her stomach, their precious secret, except of course from Dr. Walker who confirmed Savannah's good health just that morning.

Alexander, now a year old, sat on a blanket with Evelyn

and Abigail's children and an older girl who declared she was adopting him when she turned ten. The sweet miracle came into their lives because of his mother's love and sacrifice, and he continued to bring joy into every moment of every day. He had his mother's blond curls and blue eyes, and she was told by Taylor, his father's chin. Alexander clapped his hands and screeched happily at a wooden ball rolling across the blanket.

Later, as the sun dipped below the snow-capped peaks, the townsfolk said their farewells, gathering leftover food and children for the walks home. Evelyn always made sure the bachelors took a healthy share of whatever food remained back to the hotel, boardinghouse, or rented room in someone's home. Savannah's contribution of a meat pie and apple tarts appealed to the crowd enough to ensure the Munros left with empty dishes.

After volunteers coordinated times to put the church back to rights the day after Christmas, Hayes and Savannah departed the church. He lifted her into their sleigh and drove the horses north of town, past the Whitcomb's house to the other side of the meadow, where Hayes had built their house, a home large enough to accommodate their growing family. He had used lumber cut and milled from the expanded mill he invested in with the Whitcombs. There was even an extra room for Elijah when the need arose. Cooper spoke highly of Elijah to the marshal, both during the Devlin brothers' trial and before, which led the marshal to drop all potential charges against Elijah—especially after one of the mine owners confirmed Elijah had been assisting him to recover his money. Marshal Pinney had even offered Elijah a job, to which Hayes's brother kindly declined. Elijah's recent letter indicated a visit in the spring. For now, he was enjoying medical school.

Once inside their house, Hayes stoked the fire in the large hearth while Savannah stood in front of the tree they'd selected, cut, and decorated together. Alexander slept in her arms until Hayes lifted him and laid him in the larger cradle he'd finished two months prior.

When she reached out to touch a wooden heart with a carved '67 in the center hanging from a center branch, the small emerald on her ring caught the firelight.

"By my count, Hayes Munro, we still have fifty-four years to go."

He chuckled, left the growing flames to breathe, and moved in behind her. "It's a good start, Savannah Munro."

Thank you for reading *Christmas in Whitcomb Springs*!

Discover more of MK's historical romantic adventures at **mkmcclintock.com**, where every story ends with happy-ever-after. Immerse yourself in worlds where men embody chivalry, women are courageous in the face of unbelievable struggle, and both dare to embrace undeniable love.

ALSO BY MK MCCLINTOCK

Montana Gallaghers
Gallagher's Pride
Gallagher's Hope
Gallagher's Choice
An Angel Called Gallagher
Journey to Hawk's Peak
Wild Montana Winds
The Healer of Briarwood
Christmas in Briarwood

Crooked Creek Series
The Women of Crooked Creek
Christmas in Crooked Creek
The Trail to Crooked Creek

British Agents
Alaina Claiborne
Blackwood Crossing
Clayton's Honor
The Ghost of Greyson Hall

McKenzie Sisters
The Case of the Copper King

And More

Hopes and Dreams in Whitcomb Springs

Christmas in Whitcomb Springs

A Home for Christmas

Christmas in the Rockies

Discover these books and more at www.mkmcclintock.com.

ABOUT THE AUTHOR

MK McClintock is an award-winning author who writes historical romantic fiction about chivalrous men and strong women who appreciate chivalry. Her stories of romance, mystery, and adventure sweep across the American West to the Victorian British Isles with places and times between and beyond. She also writes contemporary when she's in the mood. MK enjoys a quiet life in the northern Rocky Mountains.

Visit her online at www.mkmcclintock.com.

"The four interconnected short stories will have powerful appeal to readers who like an author who can cut to the chase quickly, get to the meat of the story quickly, without a lot of fluff and padding. MK McClintock knows what readers want." — Readers' Favorite on *The Women of Crooked Creek*

"What a beautiful Christmas story! I am never disappointed In reading any of your books MK. Thank you for sharing your gift of storytelling with us." — M.L. Sullivan on *Christmas in Crooked Creek*

"*Journey to Hawk's Peak* by MK McClintock is one of the most gripping and thrilling western novels that anyone will ever read. This is probably the best novel that I have yet read as a reviewer. It clicks on all cylinders—grammar, punctuation, plot, characterization, everything. This novel is a serious page-turner, and for fans of western fiction, it is a must-read." — *Readers' Favorite*

"I just finished a six-book series by MK McClintock, the Montana Gallaghers. It is honestly the best series I have ever read. Each person is developed into a star and given their own book, but all the other characters are given their own time and investment in that book. Wow! What a series. I guarantee you won't be able to stop reading. Well done MK!" — *Pioneer Hearts Reader*

"Ms. McClintock has a true genius when writing beauty to touch the heart. This holiday treat is a gift any time one needs to remember the true meaning of love!" — InD'tale Magazine on *A Home for Christmas*

"These three stories made Christmas special for my wife and I this year. We live in the Rockies, and the stories felt very real to us. Beautifully told." — *Darrel M.,* Amazon Review on *Christmas in the Rockies*

www.ingramcontent.com/pod-product-compliance
Lightning Source LLC
LaVergne TN
LVHW041612070526
838199LV00052B/3103